W9-BZK-571

PRAISE FOR *DISCERNER OF HEARTS*:

"A feast of endlessly inventive language. . . . There are people in this collection who have nothing left but their stories and the compulsion to tell. In giving them voice, Olive Senior shows herself an astute discerner of hearts."   – *Globe and Mail*

"Evocative, honest and wonderfully nuanced, these are indeed stories by one discerning in both head and heart."
                                                    – *Books in Canada*

"These [are] memorable, often gem-like stories. . . . To read these exquisite tales is to experience life in the hot, sticky clime of that beautiful Caribbean island in all its complexity, confusion, paradoxes, morality, amorality and immorality. . . . [Senior is a] truly great, world-class talent." – Victoria *Times Colonist*

"An imaginative and distinguished collection of stories that does justice to the beauty and mystery of Jamaica."
                                                    – Montreal *Gazette*

"Her style is remarkably plain, but richly accessible; seemingly ordinary prose frames extraordinary tales, all set in Jamaica. . . . Senior possesses enormous gifts and uses them to advantage."
          – George Elliott Clarke, Halifax *Chronicle-Herald*

"*Discerner of Hearts* has a cadence that is measured by hearts beating or breaking. . . . The individuals in these stories have a quiet dignity and are skilfully brought to life as much by the emotions they feel, or are incapable of feeling, as by Senior's masterful use of dialogue."   – *Edmonton Journal*

BOOKS BY OLIVE SENIOR

POETRY

Talking of Trees 1986
Gardening in the Tropics 1994

SHORT STORIES

Summer Lightning 1986
Arrival of the Snake-Woman 1989
Discerner of Hearts 1995

NON-FICTION

The Message is Change 1972
A-Z of Jamaican Heritage 1984
*Working Miracles: Women's Lives in
the English-Speaking Caribbean* 1991

Discerner of Hearts And Other Stories

OLIVE SENIOR

M&S

First published in trade paperback with flaps 1995
This trade paperback edition published 2002

National Library of Canada Cataloguing in Publication Data

Senior, Olive
Discerner of hearts

ISBN 0-7710-8053-0 (pbk.).–ISBN 0-7710-8054-9 (trade pbk.)

I. Title.

PS8587.E552D5 1995   C813'.54   C94-932691-7
PR9199.3.S46D5 1995

We acknowledge the financial support of the Government of Canada
through the Book Publishing Industry Development Program for
our publishing activities. We further acknowledge the support of the
Canada Council for the Arts and the Ontario Arts Council for our
publishing program.

Typeset by M&S, Toronto
Printed and bound in Canada

This book is printed on acid-free paper that is
100% ancient forest friendly (100% post-consumer recycled).

McClelland & Stewart Ltd.
The Canadian Publishers
481 University Avenue
Toronto, Ontario
M5G 2E9
www.mcclelland.com

I   2   3   4   5   06   05   04   03   02

To Anna Rutherford
for helping us to sing our songs

Contents

Discerner of Hearts

Discerner of Hearts

SHE LET herself out by the back door and carefully shut it behind her, and ran through the short cut that led to the main road, hoping that no one would see. At the main road she hesitated, not because she didn't know the way but because she was terrified at what she was doing, her heart was thumping loudly against her chest, and because they were always being told never to walk on the road alone. They could get killed, Mama said, everyone drove so fast. Because of the Blackartman, Cissy said. Cissy never tired of talking about the Blackartman who drove up and down in a car and snatched children. That's why, Cissy said, you must never get into a car with a strange man, no matter how heavily it's raining or anything. Because you can never tell just by looking whether or not he is the Blackartman.

"What does the Blackartman do when he's snatched you, Cissy?" they would ask.

"He take you home and cut out your heart."

"And what does he do with your heart?"

Cissy always looked around carefully when they got to this part before leaning forward and whispering, "He want it to *use*."

"Use for what?"

But after that, Cissy's mouth clamped shut. No matter how hard they tried, they could never get her to say more. If they pressed too much, she would become sullen and serious and say, "Not good thing to talk about," and leave them to go about her business.

Because they liked being around Cissy, liked hearing her talk about her life, all the things she knew which were different from the things Mama knew, they never pressed her about the Blackartman. But they believed her, knew he was there, waiting to snatch whichever one dared to go on the road alone. Yet here she was in the bright sunlight, standing alone by the main road waiting to cross it, clutching a shiny new sixpence in her hand. She looked to both sides and, when there were no cars in sight, ran across the road and headed for Mister Burnham's house.

She knew the house well because it wasn't far from where they lived, and when Cissy took them for walks she often stopped to chat to Mrs. Burnham. She would stand by the gate let into the thick shoeblack hedge growing in front of a tall split bamboo fence which went all the way around the yard. They never went inside, though they were intensely curious.

Mister Burnham's yard was like no other. For one thing, it had any number of poles which towered above the house and from which flew squares of cloth like flags. The ones that were up for a long time got tattered and torn and the colours washed out in the sunlight, but then new flags were always going up. Aside from the flags which signalled the yard from afar, and the zinc roof of the house above the fence, they couldn't see much else. They always tried to peek through the gate as Mrs. Burnham stood behind it talking to Cissy, but Mrs. Burnham always stood close to the gate and leaned over it with her large arms crossed and Cissy stood close as she faced her. Since they were both very broad, there was little room left to peep around or between them. Cissy said it wasn't good manners to peep inside people's yards, how would you like them peeping into yours? But people were always staring openly into their yard. And Mister Burnham's wasn't just any yard: apart from the flags, sometimes behind the hedge they heard the cooing of doves, and occasionally while they watched, entranced, a large flock of white birds would rise from the back yard and circle several times before flying west.

When they asked Cissy about the flags, she said how else would you know it was a balmyard? How else could *they* find the place?

"Who are *they*, Cissy?"

"You don't worry bout *them*. You faas too much. What you don't know can't hurt you. Not everything good to eat good to talk."

"What's a balmyard, Cissy?"

"Where people go for healing."

"What is healing?"

"What people need when they have sickness."

"Why they don't go to Dr. Carter?"

"There is sick, and then again there is sick."

"But Mister Burnham isn't a doctor."

"There is doctor and there is doctor."

When Cissy carried on like that, they knew it was no use pressing her. She would just get mad and flounce off or chase them away so loudly that Mama would call out for them to stop annoying her and let her get on with her work. All they ever got out of her was that Mister Burnham — whom she called Father because that was what he was called — was a special kind of healer and that many people went to him when they had troubles. "Father Burnham a great healer. A famous man. Father have the *key*. People come from all over the world to beg Father *read* them," Cissy would boast.

They knew that wasn't possible because Mister Burnham couldn't read; like everyone else, he always came to their father for help with filling out forms or writing letters to the government or reading letters from the government, which were the only kinds of letters most people received. But they didn't bother to point this out because Cissy couldn't read either and she was extremely sensitive about the subject.

Sometimes she would pick up one of their books and hold it up, pretending to read, and if anyone pointed out that she was holding it upside-down, she got so mad. "Eh. Just because my skin black, people think I am idiot, eh? People think I fool. Just because I couldn't get to go to school like *some* backra people children, because I had was to stay home and help *my* mother look after the baby them. Never born turn-skin and rich like *some* people, couldn't get to sit round like princess, every one of them, like Missis-queen herself, and can't do one god-thing, spoil hog-rotten, the lot of them. Think because *some* people

4

go school they can faas and facety as they like, eh? Think is only book have learning? Ai. I wouldn't bother to tell *some* people all the things I know that they will never know. And you know why?" she would ask, suddenly eyeing each of them in turn as they cowered, ashamed, before her. "You know why?" Arms akimbo, she would wait for an answer. But of course, none ever came. "Because," she would end triumphantly, "no book make yet that could write down everything. Learn that!" And she would fling the book across the room and stalk out. They would get terrified when Cissy carried on like that because they never really knew why she got so angry. And so nobody bothered to contradict her about Mister Burnham reading.

Whenever they got the opportunity, they would scrutinize Mister Burnham carefully to see what Cissy saw in him to make her so proud. He certainly didn't look or behave like anyone else they knew. He was a short little man with a mischievous round face and reddish eyes. He always wore a cloth cap which he touched whenever he came to their yard and loudly greeted their father and mother even before he saw them. "Morning-Justice-Morning-Mistress-and-how-is-the-morning?" he'd call out as he approached in a voice of surprising depth and richness for one so small, and in a tone that was almost mocking. "Morning-Little-Mistresses-and-how-the-pretty-damsels-today?" he would call in a teasing voice if he caught sight of any of the children.

He came once a month to pay for the milk. His little boy Calvin came every morning with the shutpan for the quart of milk, but he himself came once a month to pay for it. They always peeped round the corner of the verandah and watched, fascinated, as he pulled a thread-bag from inside his shirt, the way a higgler would pull hers from her bosom, and poured from it onto the table in front of their father a stream of bright, shiny sixpences.

"You old reprobate," their father would laugh and, without counting the coins, he would scoop them into a paper bag from the bank.

Mister Burnham would laugh heartily too, hang his empty thread-bag around his neck and tuck it into his shirt, and if he had no other business he would touch his cap, call out, "Good day, Justice," and leave, their father's laugh ringing out after him.

Their father always seemed amused by Mister Burnham, called him "the old reprobate" both behind his back and to his face, sometimes teased him by calling out as he arrived: "Wait! Burnham, you still walking about free? Inspector don't lock you up yet?" or "Black Maria don't come for you yet?"

Mister Burnham's merry smile never wavered. "What for, Justice?"

"You damn well know what for, you scoundrel. You wait! Every day bucket go to well. . . . One day, you're going to send and beg me to run and bring these same sixpence to bail you out. But, Burnham, I couldn't do that. They would use them as evidence against you, man."

Mister Burnham would laugh along with their father till his eyes squeezed shut. "Lawd, Justice, you love make joke, eh? But you know the righteous have nothing to fear." And he would pour out his stream of bright silver sixpences and go laughing from the yard and Calvin would bring the shutpan every morning for more milk.

Sometimes in their play the girls would mimic Mister Burnham, cap on head, walking his staggering walk, pulling out his thread-bag – "And-how-are-the-Little-Mistresses?" Although Cissy would laugh at their imitations of everyone else, she never liked it when they poked fun at Mister Burnham.

"Hm. You can gwan run joke. Think Father is man to run joke bout? Father is serious man. But you is just like yu father. Have no respect for people. Unless their skin turn and they live in big house and they drive up in big car. But one day, one day the world going spin the other way though. And then we will see."

— —

Of the three of them, Theresa, the middle one, was the only one Cissy would say a lot more to, when they were alone, because she liked Theresa the best. Theresa didn't get uppity and proud and facety sometimes like Jane, the eldest, Cissy often told her friends, and she wasn't spoilt and whining and tattletale like the little one, Maud. Plus, you could say Theresa had been born into Cissy's hands, for Cissy's mother had sent her to work for the Randolphs the month before Theresa was born. Cissy was only fourteen then, and she loved the baby passionately, treated her as if she was her own.

Theresa was the only person Cissy allowed into her quarters. Nearly every afternoon, Theresa would sneak across the back yard to the little one-room cottage beneath the bread-fruit tree where she knew Cissy would be resting in the hour or two before she had to head back to the kitchen to cook dinner. Nobody knew Theresa was in Cissy's room, for she was always going off by herself and hiding in inconvenient places. Sometimes it would take the combined efforts of the entire household to search for her and most of the time they would give up, since Theresa had the habit of keeping absolutely still when it suited her. They'd be standing beneath the breadfruit tree and she'd be up in the tree, right above their heads, but so unmoving, nobody would spot her. "Theresa. Theresa!" they would call. And Theresa would sit perfectly still, reading her book up in the small breadfruit tree, or in the crotch of the orange tree at the bottom of the garden, or under the house, or behind the tank, or snugly inside the chocho arbour, for she was not afraid of lizards, as the rest of them were. Or she would be in Cissy's room.

She wouldn't answer until they all gave up, but by then they would have forgotten what they wanted her for. They wouldn't dare call out to ask Cissy if she'd seen her, for Cissy refused to speak to anyone when it was *her* time off. No one would even dare to go near Cissy's cottage, for she'd drawn an invisible territorial line around it which everybody respected. Except Theresa. Theresa would sit on the rickety chair at Cissy's dressing table and play with Cissy's things, her huge comb and her hair pomade, her bright pink face powder, her Khus-Khus essence, with which she doused herself whenever she went out, her string of beads, her shiny plastic handbag, her brightly coloured brooch, her earrings, which had what she said was a real diamond, her hairnets, her hat pins. She would try on Cissy's big church hat with the red cherries and green velvet leaves, admire her new shiny satin blouse. And Cissy would lie on her narrow bed and tell her things. Mainly, Cissy would talk about Fonso.

Fonso drove Mr. Rogers' truck all the way to and from Kingston and was therefore quite a catch; all the girls were after him, Cissy said, and Theresa, glimpsing his bright smile from the cab of the truck as he tootled past, thought him glamorous, too. But Cissy was the one who was going to take him away from Ermine, with whom he lived and had three children. Cissy was positive this would happen, because she had got *something* from Father that would make Fonso fall for her.

Theresa didn't see why Cissy needed to get anything to help her take Fonso away from Ermine, because Cissy was cool-dark and plump and beautiful and had hair she could wear in an upsweep when she was going out and white shoes with platform soles and straps, while Ermine was like a stick with picky-picky hair and a long mouth. "Yes," said Cissy, when Theresa pointed these things out, "but you don't see that Ermine *tie* him, how else she could get a man like Fonso?" So Cissy had to get something even stronger for binding.

Theresa was not surprised to go into Cissy's room one day and find Fonso there. After that, she could tell whenever Fonso was back from town, because even when she scratched at the door and called softly and Cissy knew it was her, Cissy wouldn't let her into her room. Theresa didn't mind though, because she could go back to Cissy's room later and hear all about her love life.

Cissy wouldn't say what Mister Burnham had given her to capture Fonso. She just laughed and said that Father was a powerful man and if you wanted anything at all, and you consulted him, he would help you to get it. Whenever Cissy was even slightly ill, or troubled, she would go to Mister Burnham, "for a *reading*," she said. Or a bath. When Theresa asked what was wrong with her good-good galvanize bathtub in the wash-house, Cissy explained that she was not talking about an ordinary bath.

"Is like a *spiritual* bath, Theresa, to wash over you and console you and draw out all the evil the devil plant in you that cause you to do wickedness, or feel faint, or get fever, or have belly-come-down pain, or lose the diamond from yu best earring somewhere on the road from church, or step on a flintstone that just lying in wait to give you bruise blood, or make you see a galliwasp."

Each bath had just the right combination of *bush* – herbs, leaves, flowers, bark, and roots – for Father collected them special for each and every one of his clients, from the seven hundred and seventy-seven growing things he had in his yard, plus (if he found it necessary) oil from the doctor-shop, sulphur to fight the devil with, clove, frankincense and myrrh. Theresa knew the names of many of the plants and treatments by heart, for Cissy would sometimes recite them like a litany, her eyes sparkling: "Jack-inna-bush and see-me-contract, oil-of-comeuppance and essence of keep-me-strength-good, oil-of-turn-them-back for yu enemy, powder of rose-of-sharon to strengthen nerves, strong back and chainey-root for gentlemen, leaf-of-life for ladies' complaint . . ."

Cissy was always buying from Theresa whatever silver six-pences she got as presents or could lay her hands on, for Mister Burnham had to be paid in silver sixpences.

"Why?" Theresa demanded to know.

But Cissy couldn't say. "That is just how it is. Have to pay Father in sixpence. Or the treatment don't work."

"How many sixpences you pay him?"

Cissy said it didn't matter. "As much as you have. Even one sixpence will do, if that is all you have. But you must have even one. Sometimes that is all I have to give Father. But him treat me same way. If you are big man now, say drive big car and come from Kingston, then you would give him plenty six-pence. For that is what you have."

She had been going to Mister Burnham for regular treat-ments for the longest while now, because she couldn't have a baby for Fonso. The fact that she was twenty-two and hadn't had a child was for Cissy the source of unimaginable discon-tent. Sometimes in the afternoons she would lie on her bed and cry while Theresa tried her best to comfort her.

"But, Cissy, what you want baby for? Baby isn't everything."

"Theresa, you too young to understand, chile. I am nothing but a mule. Everywhere I go, I know them calling me mule. Even my own mother start up bout it now. What good is a woman if she can't have pickney? Everybody else have baby but me poor soul. The girls my age, some of them have all two, three pickney. And me can't have even one little one. My own little sisters and all having pickney. Everybody except poor-me-gal."

Cissy crying in her room was a very different Cissy from the one who ruled the household. Theresa was the only one to whom she showed this side. Theresa wasn't pretty like the other two, and people were always so busy making a fuss over either the oldest or the youngest that by the time they got around to her she would feel let down, as if it were somehow her fault that she wasn't as engaging as they were.

She felt comfortable only when she was alone with Cissy. Cissy always told the truth. Cissy said things like, "Well, is true you not pretty like them other one there, but when you turn big woman you can fix yuself up. Straighten yu hair and wear lipstick and rouge and high-heel shoes. That time you can pretty up yuself, girl. Look just like them. Even better. For that Jane there kinda winji. She'll never get nice and fat for she hardly eat. Though a tell her all the time, 'Jane, man don't want no mawga gal.' And that Maudie? Cho. She like cry-cry too much. Bound to spoil her countenance. Furthermore," Cissy would say, "you have good-mind, you hear, better than all of them put together. You are a good girl, Theresa, for you know how to treat people like them is people. Me tell everybody seh, you are my girl, the bestest of the lot."

She would glow under Cissy's compliments and bear her truths, especially since no matter how hard Cissy was, she was always encouraging in some way. What she couldn't bear was Mama always trying to make her feel better and making her feel worse, because she knew that what she said wasn't true. "But dear, you are just as pretty and sweet as Jane. All my girls are pretty." And because she wasn't sweet and pretty, she knew, she always seemed to be doing the wrong things. She would break glasses and knock over vases and spill ink and make a mess and tear her hems down and lose her schoolbooks and forget what Mama asked her to do and just generally cause everyone to get annoyed with her about something.

"Theresa!" people were always shouting. And she knew she had done, or failed to do, something again.

Sometimes she made Mama so cross. Mama was always talking about it when Mrs. Miller or any of the other neighbours visited. "Jane is the neatest child in the world and Maud takes after her. But Theresa! My goodness, within one minute of entering a room that child has it looking like a hurricane hit." Or, "Maud is the lovingest child imaginable. Every morning she brings me little wildflowers from the garden. She picks them for me and I have to arrange them in this tiny vase. It makes her so proud. She is the kindest, most affectionate child." She didn't say, "But Theresa . . .," but Theresa knew she didn't appear as loving as the other girls, was too shy to go and bury her head in Mama's lap and throw her arms about her or leap into her father's arms as he arrived home, hung back where they came forward, kept to herself most of the time, hid away or sat in dark corners until somebody forcibly dragged her into the family circle.

———

Cissy began to fret to Theresa and shouted and yelled at all three of them for the slightest thing, slammed down the pots and pans in the kitchen, kicked at the dog, and Theresa wished that Mister Burnham would hurry up and let her have a baby.

Then one day, Theresa heard Cissy humming as she dusted,

something she hadn't done for a long while, and Cissy whispered to her as she passed, "Lizard drop on me," and laughed. Normally, Cissy was as terrified of lizards as all the other women about. Theresa couldn't understand why because she herself thought lizards were shy little creatures, but everyone knew that a croaking lizard losing its grip on the ceiling and dropping onto a woman meant only one thing.

From the minute Cissy knew she was going to have a baby, she was a transformed woman, was back to the old self they knew and loved, laughed a lot and sang and told them Anansi and Duppy stories at night, even played Johnny-coopa-lantan with the coconut brush as she shined the floor. Cissy grew happier and more beautiful as the days passed – and fatter. Eventually Mama noticed something and called her into her bedroom and locked the door and could be heard raising her voice to her, something she didn't normally do.

"Imagine," she could be heard telling their father that night. "Imagine, after all we've done for her, Cissy has turned out just like all the other girls around here. All any of them ever want to do is make baby. Imagine. We take her to church, christen and confirm her. She promised to be such a good girl, and I thought she was good, never wanted to go out at night and run around like the rest of them, and now look at what she's been doing behind my back. God knows what her mother will say. She'll swear we haven't been taking good care of her."

Mama was even more vexed when she finally got Cissy to confess who the baby was for.

"Imagine," she told their father, "that Fonso Tomlinson. That ram goat. Sweet-mouth every one of the young girls around. Fall every one of them. Every girl around here has a baby for him. And now Cissy."

Mama could often be heard lecturing Cissy now. "Well, Miss, see what happens when you're careless? I hope you'll learn your lesson." Yet each day Mama would go digging in trunks and boxes to find all her old baby things for Cissy. And she got Marse Dick, the carpenter, to come and fix and paint up the old crib, and she made Cissy two dresses with lace edging around the collars for when she got really big.

Cissy didn't care about Mama's warnings and lectures. Nor did she pay any attention to Mama's orders that she should go and register with the district nurse. She did nothing of the sort, she just got bigger and more contented.

Just as Cissy's happiness had come so swiftly overnight, one day some months later it as swiftly vanished, though Theresa was the only person who really noticed. She couldn't help noticing, for Cissy had gone back to lying on her bed and crying in the afternoons.

"Cissy, what is the matter?" Theresa asked her.

But for several afternoons, Cissy said nothing, just bawled into her pillow until Theresa, getting nowhere, was forced to leave. No one but Theresa noticed the redness of her eyes as she served dinner, the heaviness of her steps.

Finally it all came out. She was never going to have the baby now, Cissy said, because that Ermine gone and obeah her.

"Lawd, Theresa. Ermine get a obeah so bad that I will never

have baby again. Lawd Jesus, Theresa. My inside turning to ashes."

"But why?" Theresa asked. "Plenty other people have baby for Fonso that Ermine know about, and she don't do them anything."

"Yes, but that Ermine mussa find out seh Fonso going take *me* to town. Once I have the baby, Fonso going carry me and the baby to Kingston, set we up in our own room there. Once he do that, that Ermine know Fonso would never bother with the like of she again."

Theresa felt hurt by the fact that Cissy was planning to leave her, yet hadn't mentioned a single thing, but the word obeah put everything else out of her mind. The thought of obeah caused her to shiver the same way the thought of the Blackart-man did, for, said Cissy, they were one and the same, the worst thing in the whole wide world. Not even good to talk about. Now here was Ermine working obeah on Cissy.

Once, Theresa had heard her parents talking about Mister Burnham, heard her mother refer to him as "that obeahman," and was startled and frightened to have the terrifying word associated with the kindly faced, smiling Mister Burnham they knew. Was Mister Burnham also then a Blackartman? She had rushed to ask Cissy, even though it was night and they were all supposed to be in bed. Cissy was outraged.

"Shame on you, Theresa, to even say such a thing. I should wash out your mouth for you with soap, Miss. Father Burnham a obeahman? So yu mother say? Is yu father she get it from, sure as day. Is what I telling you all along, you know. Just because yu skin turn and you live in big house and drive big car, you don't know everything. Father Burnham is a good man. A *bush* man. He only deal in growing things, things that natural – bush and root and herb and what come from doctor-shop. He don't deal with dead thing – blood and feather and grave dirt and all them sinting. Father spend his whole time counteracting wickedness that obeahman do. If obeahman put it on, Father will take it off."

So now that Cissy said she was obeahed, Theresa asked her, "What you worrying for, Cissy? Just get Mister Burnham to take it off."

But this caused Cissy to weep anew. "Oh, Theresa," she cried. "You are just an innocent chile. The world don't go easy so, you know." And she turned her head to the wall again for a fresh bout of weeping. Eventually it came out. Some obeah was just too powerful even for Mister Burnham. And this was such an obeah.

"How do you know?" Theresa asked. "That's what Mister Burnham tell you?"

"No. I don't even have to go to Father. I just know. Only one man in the whole world work them kind of thing. French obeah. As you look at it you know. Is Haiti fe him mother did come from. A real Madame. Everybody know that. And fe her father was the seventh son of a seventh son and could fly straight to Africa and back in one living second. As you blink yu eye, me a tell you. Nothing can stand against that."

Cissy absolutely refused to say anything more about the obeah, though Theresa knew it must have been something she found outside her room when she woke one morning, or on the path to the water tank, maybe, or when she went to pick chochos or hang out the washing on the line. Something placed where only Cissy would find it, and know it was meant for her. Theresa was so frightened she was glad that Cissy refused to talk any more about it.

But each day Theresa could see Cissy looking wilder and more scared, her eyes becoming more sunken and shadowed. She began to lose weight, she became nervous and irritable, started forgetting things, smashing dishes, dropping pots of food. They heard Mama saying to their father that Cissy was having a serious case of nerves, but it wasn't until the day Cissy actually fainted, dropped *boof* as she walked across the yard, that Mama took matters in hand. She bundled Cissy up and got Papa to drive them to Dr. Carter. Dr. Carter spent a long time examining her but he couldn't find a single thing wrong with Cissy or the baby. "First-time nerves," he said, and packed her off with something to calm her down.

Cissy didn't believe him. "But, Cissy," Theresa kept telling her, "he says the baby's all right. Mama says he told her that you and the baby all right. See, nothing wrong with you."

But Cissy knew better. She began to talk wildly to Theresa about going mad, about wandering spirits and her Aunt Millie, about how unbearable it would be not to have a child. She went about her work in a daze, her eyes unseeing, her hands shaking. And she got thinner and thinner.

Theresa kept pleading with Cissy to go and see Mister Burnham.

"How you stay so, Cissy?" she asked whenever they were alone. "Why you just don't make up your mind to go and see Mister Burnham? What you waiting for?"

"Ai, mi chile," Cissy would say, sighing and shaking her head and breaking into a fresh bout of weeping. "Girl, is not everything you understand, ya. Some things not even Father powerful enough to undo."

Theresa became so disturbed that she too began to have sleepless nights, or she slept fitfully and had terrible nightmares and would jump out of bed screaming and drenched with sweat. Her mother kept on asking her what was wrong and she kept on telling her "nothing," until she also was dragged off to Dr. Carter. "Too highly strung," he said, and prescribed something to settle *her* nerves.

One morning, during the summer vacation, Theresa woke up and knew what she had to do. It came to her just like that. If Cissy would not go to Mister Burnham, then she, Theresa, would have to go to him on her behalf. The minute she decided this, her heart felt lighter and she could hardly wait for breakfast to be over and for everyone to go about their business so she could sneak off to Mister Burnham's. She had decided not to tell anyone, not even Cissy. As soon as Theresa saw her mother settled at her sewing machine, she slipped out of the house and ran, taking the short cut to the main road, dashing across it with her heart beating wildly, to stand trembling in front of Mister Burnham's gate. She was so frightened, it took her quite a while to recover her voice and call out, "Hello. Anybody home? Hello. Mrs. Burnham?" To her own ears her voice sounded so thin she knew no one would hear her, and she shifted the silver sixpence she had carried from her right to her left hand and bent down and picked up a small stone and used it to knock on the gate. But though her knock got bolder and bolder there was no response and no sign of life inside that she could see when she peeped through the slats of the gate. Her courage began to fail and she would have turned back but, thinking of Cissy, she lifted the latch, pushed open the gate, and entered Mister Burnham's yard. She had barely shut the gate behind her when two dogs came rushing out from around the back, barking madly as she stood stock-still, too terrified to move as they bounded towards her. But as they neared, they seemed to recognize her from the earlier visits with Cissy and their barks turned to happy sniffs and wagging of tails. They followed her as she went up to the front door of the house and knocked, out of politeness, but she knew that Mrs. Burnham would have shut the door only if she were going out, and the windows were closed.

All at once the sound of doves cooing drew her to the side of the house, where she looked open-mouthed with amazement at all the things in Mister Burnham's yard. There were the flagpoles, which could be seen from the road, and the dovecotes, but there were other strange structures: tree stumps with calabash bowls perched on top of them; in some of the calabashes there were bougainvillea flowers and croton leaves, on another pole there was a strange metal object. Horseshoes were nailed up on the side of the house and on the dovecote. There were plants and bushes growing everywhere, some up against the house, at the far side a whole field of them planted out in rows, looking not at all like the plants in other people's gardens.

But what really drew her was the building right behind the house, separated from it by a clean-swept yard. She never knew it was there, for it could not be seen from the road. It was a rectangular structure, much bigger than the house itself. The narrow side nearest the house was walled in wattle-and-daub to form a room which she couldn't see into, for the windows were shuttered. It had two doors, one on the side facing the house and the other leading to the larger room, but these were also closed.

She could look right into the big room for there were no walls, only the poles which held up the roof. In the centre of the thatched roof was a small circle, open to the sky, and through it the centre pole projected. The dirt floor was tamped hard as cement, and around the centre pole strange pictures and symbols had been freshly drawn in chalk; she could see fragments of earlier pictures that had been rubbed out in the clay.

At one end, where the smaller room was located, there was a wooden platform. Every inch of the wall behind it, including the door cut into it, was covered with paintings. She recognized scenes from the Bible, Jesus and his disciples, and signs and symbols like those in her church. But these didn't look quite like the religious scenes they got on their Sunday School picture cards. For one thing, they all ran into one another with nothing to define each one, and they were much more colourful and lively. And all the people, Jesus included, were black. On a stand in front, which looked like an altar, for it had a white lace cloth draped over it, there was a large book that looked like a Bible, a large wooden cross, lots of jars with water, some with flowers and croton leaves, and rows and rows of candles.

Although she had never seen a room like this before, more and more it reminded her of a church, for rough benches were arranged in two rows in front of the platform. It seemed natural for her to go in and sit on a bench in the front row to wait for Mister Burnham. As she sat, the dogs which had been following her came in and lay at her feet. She felt very safe and peaceful there.

Now she was inside, she could see a large board nailed to a post to the left side of the platform. Someone had written all over it in white paint, the words spilling over the edges and continuing onto the next line in eccentric fashion, the letters badly formed, the spelling funny, too, as if the writer had never been taught. But, as if the person didn't care, the painted letters were jauntily decorated which swirls and squiggles and dots. She thought she recognized the drawing of a key, and, as far as she could make out, for it took her a long time to read it, the writing below it said, or was trying to say: "Come unto me all ye that are heavy laden and I will give you rest."

Below that was a drawing of a dove with a twig in its beak. Then:

> All Welcome.
> Father Burnham. M.H.C., G.M.M.W., D.D., K.R.G.D.
>> Bringer of Light.
>> Professor of Peace.
>> Restorer of Confidence.
>> Discerner of Hearts.
> Consultation and advice.

Theresa read the phrases, not understanding what all of them meant, but she was sure nevertheless they were saying something about Cissy's problems. Who more than Cissy needed Light, Peace, Confidence? She didn't know what "Discerner of Hearts" was, but she liked how the words sounded.

Just then, though she hadn't heard a sound, the dogs bounded up and Mister Burnham himself appeared through the painted door. He didn't seem at all surprised to see her, as he came and sat on the edge of the platform in front of where she sat, smiling and beaming as he always did, his short legs barely touching the ground.

"And how's the Little Mistress today?" he asked in his big booming voice.

"Well, thank you, Mister Burnham."

"The Little Mistress is troubled?" he asked in a softer voice.

"It says 'Restorer of confidence. Discerner of hearts . . .'" she started to say. She wanted to ask him what this last thing meant but suddenly she stopped. Suppose Cissy was wrong and Mister Burnham was the Blackartman. Suppose discerner meant stealing, stealing children's hearts. Her own heart was beating so loudly she was sure he could hear it, could know exactly where it was located, could simply grab it and tear it out. She desperately wanted to get up and run, but, as in the nightmares, her body felt like lead.

But Mister Burnham only said in an even softer voice: "Ah. You are the Little Mistress that can read so good. You are the bright one."

She was so surprised to hear him say this, it took some of

her fear away. Surely the Blackartman couldn't be someone who knew her? Plus, Mister Burnham didn't have a car. And he drank their milk.

"I'm Theresa," she said.

"I know. Cissy friend. Long time I don't see Cissy."

"Mister Burnham. Cissy . . . ," but she couldn't go on. Embarrassed, she held out the sixpence. He took it without comment and, pulling out his thread-bag, dropped it in.

"You want a consultation?" he asked.

"Well, not for me. For Cissy. Mister Burnham, you know bad obeah on Cissy. Ermine put it there. Mister Burnham, please do something to take the obeah off Cissy. Or else she going mad. And she's my friend. I can't let her go mad." And she burst into tears.

Mister Burnham didn't say anything but produced a newly pressed handkerchief and handed it to her. In between wiping her eyes and blowing her nose, she noticed that he was not looking at her, he was looking out the window and seemed very serious, quite unlike the clownish Mister Burnham who came to pay for the milk.

Finally he said, "I know all about Cissy."

"So you can help?"

"Perhaps. Perhaps not. Cissy own self must ask."

"But she won't come."

"Right."

She waited for him to say more about Cissy. Instead, he said, "You mustn't worry so much about those other ones, you know. You worry that you not pretty, that you don't have tall hair, that you don't hear when yu mother talk to you. You fret that nobody love you. Now, what you need to do is stop fretting. Cast yu eye around you. Look at the flowers, the clouds, the butterflies. You see them worrying? No sah. They just going about their business same way, happy to be alive. Look at you. Such a sweet little gal. You not sick. You not poor. You have a nice Mammy and Daddy to look after you. Much more than all those other children about. You are going to grow up to be a fine lady, for you have a big, big heart. But you must stop feeling bad bout yuself."

She didn't say anything but looked at him. How did he know? But then she thought, this Mister Burnham knows everything. Cissy was right. This Mister Burnham was not the silly little man who came to their yard making jokes with their father. He was not an evil man, as their mother thought. This Mister Burnham was a serious man, someone you could put your trust in.

"Cissy . . . ?" she asked.

"If you want something really bad, you see, you must make sure that it is something that good for you," he said. "Plenty time we want something bad-bad but when we get it, it stick in we craw." She wondered what that had to do with Cissy.

"Well, Little Mistress, they probably wondering what happen to you," he said briskly and stood up, and she found herself standing, too, walking with Mister Burnham out through his yard to the road. Although she had not got what she came for, she felt happy, as if relieved of a great burden. Mister Burnham held her hand and walked her across the road, and at the short cut to her yard, he wished her good day.

"Come again, Little Mistress, any time you want. You have a

friend." She set off smiling, proud to have a friend like Mister Burnham. When she had walked quite a distance, she heard him calling out to her: "Cissy. Maybe you can help Cissy. You have a big enough heart."

She started to ask him what he meant, but he was gone; and when she got back home, without anyone seeing her, she was surprised to find the silver sixpence in her hand.

Theresa kept her secret to herself all day, though she was almost bursting with excitement. She kept away from Cissy, so afraid was she of spilling the news to her at the wrong moment. She knew that the story of her visit had to be told to Cissy only when they were alone and Cissy was in the right mood to receive it.

When she finally entered Cissy's room that afternoon, she had started to talk before she even closed the door, and was gratified to see that her news made Cissy show some interest for the first time in weeks in something other than her own problem.

"You!" Cissy said. "You go alone to see Father?" She was incredulous because Theresa was the shyest person she knew; she would hide even when her own aunts and uncles came to visit. Now here was Theresa going off alone. "By yu own self. What a thing!" she exclaimed in admiration.

"Mister Burnham send you greetings," Theresa said, wondering how this could have popped into her head. "Say he long to see you till he short. Say you going to have a bouncing baby boy."

Cissy was interested despite herself. "Him really say that?"

"Weighing seven and a half pounds."

"Theresa! You taking me mek poppyshow."

"If you think a lie, spit in mi eye," Theresa boldly offered Cissy's own challenge to her.

"Well . . . a don't know." Theresa could see Cissy filling up with doubts again. "You tell him it real bad?"

"The baddest. But I didn't have to tell him. He know all about it already. Cho. Mister Burnham just laugh. Say why you don't have more faith? Say nothing put on yet that can't take off. Say you need a bath bad-bad. Need to have River Jordan wash right over you. Cleanse you of evil. Bring you light. Restore your confidence."

Theresa wondered where all of this was coming from; she knew she was not half as good a liar as Jane, yet here she was making up all these things to tell Cissy. Cissy wondered too at how Theresa could suddenly talk so well, she really sounded like Father Burnham. Perhaps she wasn't telling lies, perhaps she had been to see Father after all.

But it was an uphill battle with Cissy. For weeks she see-sawed between wanting to believe in Father Burnham and falling prey to her fright about what Ermine had put on her. Wanting to believe Theresa and remembering how her heart dropped clear to her footbottom, how she wet herself, felt that her whole insides had fallen away, when she saw it, the thing that she had stepped on. That was the worst part, if only she hadn't mashed it, had sidestepped it, then she wouldn't have seen, might have gone on unknowing, believing it was just any little thing, something she could get Father to deal with.

But her own mother had told her what to look out for, how to know, told her that time when Cissy was small and Aunt Millie had gone right off her head and the police had come in a Black Maria and taken her away in a straitjacket to Bellevue asylum. They had done something their people had never done before: asked the police to come and take one of their own to Bellevue, for there was mad and there was mad, and they knew that no power on earth could help her, so they let the white people look after her in their hospital since the Millie they knew no longer existed.

When she finally drowned herself in the hospital water tank, ripping apart the protective wire mesh with her bare hands to throw herself in, they said, "Jesus be praised." One year later, they held a memorial for her like nobody had ever seen before, dancing three nights straight to summon her to be reunited with her family. But the power that had been used on Aunt Millie was so great she couldn't find her way back, not even when the drumming went on for nine hours one time, when Isaac dropped with exhaustion and Clayton grabbed the drum without missing a beat and Isaac came back and took over from him again, for the spirits were arriving so fast the room was thick with them, spirits from everywhere, but no Millie. No matter how hard they tried to call her, Aunt Millie couldn't find her way back. To this day, her spirit hasn't rested.

After what happened to Aunt Millie, Cissy's mother had taken her to get an extra powerful new guzu to wear around her waist, but she had also warned her that there were certain things that no guzu could protect her from, and she had to learn to be careful about everything and not offend a soul. She had to learn to live right.

Which is exactly what Cissy used to tell Theresa all the time when Theresa was small.

"Theresa," she would say, faithfully repeating what her own mother had taught her, "never, never fling water outa door like that when you done wash yu face at night." Theresa had a slop pail, part of the pretty china set on her washstand, but she never used it, preferring the big-people feeling it gave her to open the window wide and lift up the basin and dash the water outside.

"I keep telling you, you suppose to be polite at all times to them Ol'People, for if they be good people, only their body leave this earth, their spirit come back after the nine night and they right out there, protecting you," Cissy would patiently explain. "If you treat them good, and show respect, and feed them now and then, they will look out for you, keep you from harm's way. That's why I keep telling you, Theresa, never fling anything outa door without first say, 'Ol'People: mind yuself,' so they can get out of the way. For you wouldn't feel insult and want to do bad things to somebody who fling cold dutty water in yu face that way?"

But Theresa never seemed to pay any attention to Cissy's warnings and, after a while, Cissy stopped worrying about her, for it came to her one day that people like Theresa didn't need that kind of protecting for nothing seemed to threaten them, people with their turn-skin and big house and big car. They were born protected. It was only people like her who needed charms and baths, ceremonies and drums to protect them, who needed to be so careful, to live good in the world, for there was nothing else between them and the night, between them and the whole world full of dangers out there, nothing else to fight off straitjacket and Bellevue. No big house with electric light to drive away duppies at night, no big car to whisk them safely past dark corners and crossroads where Rolling Calf and Three-Foot-Horse waiting for every poor black sinner forced to walk foot.

So Cissy ignored Theresa's breaches of etiquette and carried on as her own mother had taught her: Never spill salt without flinging a pinch behind you. Don't talk loud at night or duppy will catch yu voice. If you want to gaze at full moon, look at it in a basin of water. Always walk with corn grain or rice to throw in case Rolling Calf follow you. Don't comb yu hair at night for it will make you forgetful. Wrap knife and fork in a page of the Bible and sleep with it under yu pillow to keep evil spirit away. Don't walk backwards or you will curse yu parents. Don't throw fingernail cutting and hair from comb away careless; hide and bury them, or people will use them against you.

And Cissy always remembered to tread carefully, day or night, as she went about her business, in order to sidestep certain things, should you happen to make somebody grudgeful enough to put them in your way. For, if you didn't, no power on earth could save you from what befell Aunt Millie.

Theresa thought she could see a change of some sort in Cissy, and it made her try harder.

"Mister Burnham, that day I went to see him, say he see you big woman with five sons. And two daughters," she would say casually as she played with Cissy's beads. If that got no response, she was amazed to find that she could continue talking. "Say you make to have children. Say you'll have them easy, too. You will have children and grandchildren around you in your old age. To play with my children and grandchildren."

"Father never say that!" Cissy would angrily protest. "You too young to know anything bout having children."

Theresa would laugh and say, "No, I made that part up." And occasionally, now, Cissy would laugh along with her.

Cissy desperately wanted to believe that what Theresa was telling her was true; desperately wanted to be able to go to Father Burnham and have him take this heavy burden off her and give her peace. She didn't want to die or go mad like Aunt Millie, didn't want to become a wandering spirit. Suppose her mother wasn't always right? After all, Father had helped her many times before, been like a true father to her from the time she left her mother's house as a young girl. And her mother was far away: she hadn't seen her for a long time now. What did she have to lose by going to get a bath from Father Burnham?

Maybe she needed more than a bath. Maybe Father would arrange a special ceremony for her. She could request a Table, a feast to placate the spirits and beg their forgiveness with danc-ing and singing and drumming. If everything went well, the ancestors would answer the drums, their spirits would come and dance through their children. She felt lightheaded as she thought of the drums talking to the spirits, calling them down, of the nights she had crept out when everyone was asleep to go to Father's yard, danced and fallen into the spirit herself, got home as dawn was breaking. Tired, yes, but ready for the night to come again so she could dance and catch the spirit summoned by the drums at Father Burnham's yard.

But her mind was only fully made up the day Theresa casually said, "You know Mister Burnham did even know what Ermine set on you?" What had Theresa said? Cissy was so shocked she couldn't speak. She had never breathed to a soul what she had seen on the path that day, what her own mother told her to watch out for. Yet Father had known. How could he?

"Theresa, Theresa girl, tell me true. Father did really say so, or you joking?"

"Cissy, you think I could joke about a serious thing like that? Mister Burnham told me he know. I didn't ask him. And Cissy" – Theresa was feeling inspired now – "he say he know what he going to have to put in the bath to counteract it."

"What you saying?"

"Well, he did tell me, he call plenty name, but it's too much for me to remember. I only remember it was seven times seven different bushes and roots and herbs, Mister Burnham said, mix with nine different oil from doctor-shop."

Cissy was convinced now that Theresa couldn't have made that up, because she had known Father to use exactly that kind of recipe to drive out a troublesome duppy that was causing rockstone to fall on a house and pots to go flying off the fire and dishes to smash into the wall and the people inside to run for their lives. Father was particularly proud of that case for it was a celebrated one. It had even been written up in the *Gleaner*, and many learned men from the university had gone down to the house where this was happening to see what they could do. But nobody could do anything, the duppy even chased out the university men, flung stones at their car, caused one to drop his briefcase and another to lose a sandal as they rushed to get away. Nobody could do anything until Father Burnham was called in, but there was nothing in the *Gleaner* about that, for this thing had gone on too long and people had lost interest.

Father Burnham had right away traced the cause to a young boy living in the house. He had had to use all his powers to get rid of the duppy which had taken up residence inside him. He had been proud of that case. It was the toughest he had ever had, he said, it was such a troublesome duppy. But he chased that duppy so well, the people were never troubled again and could go back to their home. Although Father was not a boastful man, one Sunday afternoon when Cissy was there, he couldn't help talking about it to her and Mrs. Burnham, he was so pleased. "Seven time seven bush root and herb I had was to use. The highest remedy for the baddest cause. Pick them myself. Oh, that was a tough one. Seven time seven and nine different oil from the doctor-shop."

How could Theresa know about this, Cissy wondered, unless she had got it straight from Father Burnham?

Cissy decided that she didn't want to go mad, or have her womb turn to ashes, or die, or turn into a wandering spirit, if Father could prevent it, and he seemed to think he could. She wanted to get better and she wanted to have her baby. She would go to him.

Once she decided, she felt a lightening of her spirits, a quickening of her body, as if the baby was still alive. But she didn't think about that. She didn't want to hope too much.

Yet she kept putting off going, as if she were bothered by something else. And she finally had to admit that she was ashamed to go to Father, she'd been ashamed from the start, for in a way she knew she had brought the evil on herself. Her mother had taught her to live right and not offend a soul: Don't act better than other people. Don't be grudgeful and don't cause other people to grudgeful you. For grudgefulness will cause spite and cut-eye and bring you more than you can handle.

And hadn't she herself attracted Ermine's wrath? She had to admit now, she never suspected that Ermine had it in her to get such a bad obeah, she had seriously miscalculated that little dryfoot girl. But she had grudged Ermine her man, taken him away, was going off to Kingston with him even, and that had caused Ermine to turn around and grudge her. As for the man himself, for the first time she realized that she hadn't seen Fonso once since Ermine obeah her. Imagine that. He would have known what Ermine had done, for she would be sure to tell him. And that had been enough to keep him away.

Cissy had been ashamed to go to Father Burnham because she had sorely deceived him. When she went to get something to get her man, he didn't ask who it was, but because he was like a real father to her, he said, "I only hope his name don't begin with the letter F. For I could never encourage you with that at all." And she had lied and said, no, his name began with the letter D. And Father had believed her, for he had given her the charm. But now he knew she had lied, and it was Fonso after all.

The whole thing served her right, Cissy told herself, for if she hadn't been thinking about Fonso that day, hadn't been actually smiling to herself when she thought of Fonso and herself cozy-up together in their own room, in Kingston, she would never have mashed the thing Ermine put in her way, her mind would have been clear as it always was, on the lookout for just that kind of trouble, and she would have been able to sidestep it. That Fonso was the cause of all her troubles.

When it came down to it, she didn't care now if she never saw him again. He could go back to long-mouth Ermine and his other baby mothers. She didn't even want a room in Kingston. "What I want room in Kingston for when I have good-good room right here where I can raise baby?" she asked herself. A son, Father had said, seven and a half pounds.

Cissy screwed up her courage and went to Father Burnham, and Father could look into her heart and discern that it was pure again, so he gave her the bath with seven times seven bushes, roots, and herbs. And he said, yes, if she wanted, he could arrange a Table for her. Soon, soon, she begged, for the baby was getting bigger and kicking like mad.

Cissy told Theresa about her visit to Father Burnham and what was in the bath he gave her and how she had decided to give up Fonso and have the baby right there and what kind of guzu she would get for the boy and what she was going to name him though she changed her mind every day and how she would take him to church to be christened by the parson because you couldn't have too much protection in this world and how Theresa would be his godmother and would have to teach him his ABC as soon as he was old enough, before he went to school.

But there were some things she didn't tell Theresa. For although Theresa was her friend and had a big heart, she knew that her kind of people wouldn't understand why someone like her could take the last farthing she had to her name, everything hidden under the floorboard, and give it all to Father Burnham to pay the drummers and prepare for the feast: buy goat and white rooster, rice to cook without salt, rum and showbread and condensed milk for the chocolate tea, candles and everything else for the Table.

Theresa wouldn't understand how badly she needed to be there in Father's yard with everything set up just so, the Table laid with the showbread and the fruit, the candles, the water and the rum, the Bible and the flowers, incense, frankincense and myrrh. The right signs on the floor and the fresh new flag flying to attract the right spirits down the pole. Wouldn't know how badly she needed to be with her own people dressed all in blue robes for cutting and clearing, Sister Brooks with her scissors for cutting away evil, Brother Thom with his whip for driving out devils, Shepherd Casey the warrior with his sword to guard the door, Sister Icilda who cooed like a dove, all her own people feasting and praying and singing with her. And the drums finally calling down the spirits, inviting the ancestors to enter, to possess, to shower her and her son with blessings.

— —

Everyone was surprised by the change in Theresa. Overnight, she seemed to have lost her shyness. Didn't hide away so much, chatted more, hugged her mother every now and then, ran with the other girls to greet her father as he came in, didn't seem as clumsy as she used to be, looked at herself in the mirror almost as often as Jane.

"She's growing up," her mother could be heard telling their father.

Much to their astonishment, when next Mister Burnham came to pay for the milk, she ran out from the side verandah, where the girls usually hid to giggle as they watched him pour out silver sixpences, and rushed to greet him at the gate before he even opened his mouth. "Good morning, *Father* Burnham," she called in her strong new voice. Everyone was amazed to see her chatting away with Mister Burnham as if they were the oldest of friends, to see her proudly walk with him on to the verandah where her father sat, as if she were ushering in an honoured guest.

The Case Against the Queen

EVERY AFTERNOON just before four o'clock, Uncle got ready to go out. Not that he needed much preparation. He had not taken off his three-piece suit since he came from England, so all he had to do was put on his bowler hat and take up his walking-stick and his gloves. But even these simple actions were imbued with great purpose and deliberation, as was everything that Uncle did. His hat set at the right angle, his gloves in his right hand precisely delineated in relation to his cane, he would set out.

"Good afternoon to you, Girlie," he would call out in his deep, melodious voice.

"Good afternoon, Uncle," I would say, coming out of my bedroom, where I was studying, to watch him setting off.

Ramrod stiff, Uncle would walk down the three concrete steps onto the path to the road, never missing a beat, behaving exactly, I was sure, as if he were going for a walk in Piccadilly Circus. The only difference was that there was no pavement on our country road; in fact, there wasn't much of a road, only a track covered with stones and marl with no drainage so the sides of the road were deeply rutted from the water which found channels there every time it rained. It was a good thing there was so little traffic, because the only place to walk was in the middle of the road.

None of this seemed to bother Uncle. He would step into the road, swinging his cane, heedless of what the sharp rocks were doing to his highly polished English shoes or of the dust from the marl clinging to his clothes. Stepping stiffly and precisely, he would walk the mile and a half to the village square, lifting his hat in greeting to everyone he passed, smiling his smile that never wavered because it was fixed on his face, turned forever inward. Sometimes if I happened to be down at the square, I would catch sight of him there. He would walk down one side, turn precisely at the corner, cross the road, and come up the other side and head for home again, resisting with a slight inclination of his head the blandishments of the men inside the bar – Grampa's friends – to come in and have a drink. Uncle would simply smile his smile, nod, and pass on; he never spoke to anyone on his walk.

Uncle walked so stiffly, he always reminded me of the little wind-up toy man I once had which moved with a mechanical jerk of its hands and feet. He held himself stiffly at all times, even when he was sitting down. I had never once seen him relax his posture, as none of us had ever seen him out of his three-piece suit.

For the first few days after Uncle came back from England, nobody thought too much about his behaviour. Everyone knew that he would need time to adjust to being back home after twenty years, and expected that as soon as the stiffness and strangeness wore off, Uncle would start behaving like a normal person again. From the start, though, Gran had tried to get him to take off his suit and his vest and his tie; she couldn't imagine how he wasn't boiling in those heavy black English woollen clothes, she said. She hadn't seen any other clothes, because although he came back with a trunk, he hadn't taken anything out of it except pyjamas and a robe, toilet articles, and a fancy comb and brush set, and he kept the trunk locked. She had offered to unpack his things, air out and hang up his clothes, and iron what needed ironing. "No, thank you, Mother," he said. She did try again by offering him one of his father's cambric shirts and khaki pants to put on, as well as a pair of his shoes, for they still wore the same size, thinking perhaps that he had no tropical clothing, but again he said, "No, thank you, Mother," and that was that. His voice was fruity and melodious, so cultured, so precise, I thought, as if he formed the words around a ripe plum in his mouth. "No, thank you," was all he ever said but I loved to hear him say even that.

"Take him a little time to unwind and get used to our ways again," I heard Gran telling Grampa every night. "Soon get back to normal."

Grampa didn't answer. Grampa wasn't used to saying much except on Friday nights when he went down to Mr. Ramsay's bar and drank white rum. Then he became loquacious enough, noisy even, and could sometimes be heard loudly arguing with his friend Mr. Anderson as, late at night, they both staggered up the road, drunk. Through the wall dividing our rooms I could hear Gran (who would be lying in bed listening) sigh loudly. I could imagine her shaking her head as she got out of bed to turn up the lamp which she always left burning low when Grampa was away. I would see through the open doorway the sudden glow and hear her hurry back into bed so she could pretend to be asleep when Grampa came staggering in. She never said anything to him about Friday nights because, other than that, he didn't give her much to complain about. "Not like when we were young. Oh boy," she would say. "That man made me cry the living eye-water every day." But Grampa had mellowed with age and now hardly spoke at all. Uncle didn't speak either, unless he was spoken to. Then, regardless of what was said or offered, he would say, "No, thank you."

I was the only one to whom Uncle said anything more and I never knew why. Gran had told me he had been close to my mother before he went away and I was the spitting image of her. I never knew if this was so or not, because she died when I was a baby and the only photograph Gran had of her was a snapshot that was so pale, so worn, I couldn't make out her features. Sometimes I wondered if Uncle thought I was the little sister he had left behind when he went to England, for they'd called her Girlie, too.

When Uncle had first come back to live with us the year I was ten, I was intensely curious about him and I would hang around the verandah where he sat, ramrod stiff, hoping he would say something to me. He sat on the chair all day long, smiling his secret smile, never relaxing his pose until Gran called him to the table for a meal. Then he would come and sit at the table and go through the pretence of eating, for hardly anything ever passed his lips.

For a long time he never gave any indication that he noticed me at all. Then one afternoon as I was passing his door I was astonished to hear him call out, "Come here, Girlie, and listen to my heart."

Feeling somewhat embarrassed, I went and pressed my ear to his chest.

"What do you hear?" he asked.

"It's beating, Uncle," I said, for what else was there to say?

"No, Girlie, you are wrong," he said. "That's not my heart you hear beating. I don't have a heart any more. That's a mechanical contrivance they put inside of me. Ticking like a clock. They took my heart out when I went into hospital there. The doctors attached some wires to my head and when I was unconscious they took my heart out and put in this machine. I never asked them to do that, Girlie. I never asked them. It was advantage-taking to the highest degree. I wrote to the Queen about it. Forty letters I wrote to the Queen. And you know what the Queen wrote me back to say?"

He was waiting for a response so I dutifully said, "No, Uncle."

"The Queen, Girlie, wrote back to say it was none of her business. Can you countenance that? Isn't she supposed to be the Queen of us all down to the humblest? Don't we all walk with money in our pockets with her face on it? Millions and millions of people all over the world carrying her face in their pockets. And then to say it is none of her business that *her* doctors in *her* hospital – *Royal* it says in large letters outside for everyone to see – her doctors take away my heart and put a clock inside. You think that is right, Girlie? I have to be careful how I drink, you know. For the rest of my life I have to be careful. For suppose the machine they put inside of me starts to rust? But I'll never give up, Girlie. If I have to spend my whole life seeking justice, that I will do. One day I will show you my entire correspondence with the Queen."

"Yes, Uncle," I said.

Uncle pulled his watch out of his fob pocket, looked at it, and, since it was precisely one minute to four, he put his hat on his head, took up his gloves and his walking-stick. "Good afternoon to you, Girlie," he said and he set off on his walk.

When I told Gran what Uncle had told me, she burst into tears. "Poor Sonny. Poor Sonny," she said. "What a way life hard, eh?"

Grampa didn't want to talk about their son but Gran was always trying to get him to do so, but Grampa wouldn't say anything, although we knew he was embarrassed. Wasn't this the son he had boasted about for twenty years? When he heard Uncle was finally coming home, hadn't he bought a round for everyone in the bar that Friday night? Hadn't they all bought him a round? Hadn't Grampa got so drunk from the celebration he had to be carried home?

Grampa was extraordinarily proud of his son because while everyone had sons or daughters overseas they were always bragging about, his son was the one with the brains, he had been saying that for twenty years, the one who was always studying. Mark you, Grampa used to get a bit vague about the studying. Uncle had left to study medicine. Many, many years he spent studying. Nobody knew what happened but nothing seemed to come of it. Next thing they knew, he was studying something else. Every time they heard, he was studying something different. After a while, Grampa and Gran never really knew what Uncle did, for he hardly ever wrote home. They didn't even know that Uncle had a wife and children until this strange woman named Clarissa wrote to say Uncle was ill and in hospital. She didn't specify the nature of the illness and the name of the hospital meant nothing to them. After that they heard from her occasionally though she never specifically acknowledged any of their letters; she wrote more to express her feelings at any given point in time than to assuage theirs. He was in and out of hospital, she was having a hard time with the children, well, poor Sonny was never much good for anything, was he? Grampa and Gran didn't know what to make of that, so they pretended they hadn't read it.

All along, Grampa pretended; he was always announcing good news of his son, boasting of his grandchildren and their achievements. Everyone knew he was pretending since who got letters from abroad and who didn't was a secret shared with all by Postmistress, but nobody ever let him know that they knew for a lot of people with children overseas had had to resort to the same type of face-saving from time to time. It was just that Grampa had been doing it for longer than most. Over the years, he continued to make up news of his son to pass on to his bar cronies. And they went and dutifully told their wives as if it were gospel truth, so then Gran had to end up lying as well. For the ladies would say to her after church, "My, my, Miss Margaret. I hear Sonny get another big job, eh?"

"Well, yes, Miss Dorcas," she'd say, "you can't keep a good man down."

But Gran would try to hurry off before the discussion got too deep, because she never knew what news Grampa had manufactured about Uncle this time and she was afraid of getting it all wrong. She didn't quarrel with Grampa because a man had to have something to boast about and others in the district were always making them so angry, what with their children coming home or sending them gifts. Every day somebody would pass by on the road with something or other they had got from foreign, just to torment them, it seemed. The boys would walk with their shirtsleeves rolled up to show off new wristwatches, the girls would wear their new high-heel shoes, they'd walk with radios to their ears, and one silly girl even tried to push her baby in a pram down the rocky road, sent by her equally silly sister from Birmingham. It was worse when new things came in: television sets (even before they had electricity, or, indeed, a television station), refrigerators, and stereograms. Not to mention all their fancy clothing, new curtains and bedspreads.

Grampa and Gran were embarrassed that they had never got anything from their son abroad. So when Uncle's wife wrote and said she was sending him home because she couldn't do any more, they went off to meet him still hoping against hope that he would bring them many and various gifts to make up for all the years of deprivation. It wasn't that they really wanted anything. It was a matter of principle; they needed things to show off with. Just like everybody else.

Before Uncle came home, Gran used to hold him up as an object lesson to me. "See there, Girlie, see where you can reach if you study and apply yourself. Reach to England. Go all to university like your Uncle Sonny. You stick to the books there, girl." After Uncle returned with nothing but a trunk, which he kept locked, and they saw how he was, Gran changed her advice.

I don't know at what stage Gran decided that Uncle was mad, though at first she never ever used that word. What she said was that Uncle was suffering from "brain strain" which everybody knew was caused from too much studying. So whereas before she was always urging me to study, was always checking on my progress, now she worried constantly that I was overdoing it, that I too would strain my brain. "Remember what happen to your uncle," she would say from time to time. "You better pack up the books now and go to bed."

At night, though, when she talked to Grampa in their room beside mine and I listened through the wall, she was turning different theories over in her head. Those days, Gran and Grampa hardly seemed to sleep and I would be surprised to wake up and hear Gran talking in the middle of the night in her normal conversational voice. "Johnnie," she would say to Grampa, "you think we did push Sonny too hard when he was little? You think we did ask too much of him? He really never have time to play like them other little boys around, you know. He was always a serious little fellow, serious from the day he was born."

I settled down to listen to Gran, as if to keep her company, for even if Grampa were awake he would never answer her, except to grunt now and then or, if she went on too long, to say angrily, "Woman, why you don't shut up and let a man get his sleep?" Sometimes, as if she never heard him, Gran would continue to talk aloud for hours. I would try to stay awake and listen, in case Gran said something about my mother, who died when she had me so I never knew her, but Gran never talked about her except to tell me how much she cried as a baby. All I knew was what I heard Gran say when she thought nobody but Grampa was listening, but since Uncle came home he was all she talked about.

"He wasn't even a year yet when Girlie born. But Sonny never give a day's trouble, he must have known his poor mother never had no time to fuss over him," she would say. "That Girlie! She took up all my strength. The minute she get over one sickness she get another. Never know she would make it through her first two year. I never had time for that little Sonny, but I never see a child tough so. Sonny never cry. And from he was little he was helpful. Never a day's trouble. He was a perfect child."

Gran would fall silent for a while, thinking, no doubt, of her two lost children, and I would be falling asleep again when her voice would rouse me back to wakefulness.

"But, Johnnie, talk truth now. You don't think we did use

him too hard from he was little, seeing how he was the one boy pickney? Remember how he used to get up from dew-fall to go to the spring for water? Then he had was to get rabbit feeding. Then he go look wood and tie out the goat. Then he walk the five mile to school for is clear to Ramble he had to go for no school was here those days and no bus neither. Then he come home and he running around again till night dark you have to say. Then he spend half the night studying. Remember, Johnnie? And you was hard on him, you know. Used to beat him for blind for the slightest thing. Old man, your temper was well short those days."

Grampa would groan loudly from his side of the bed as if he were being tortured but Gran would ignore him. "He did always want to succeed. From he was little he would tell me, 'Mamie, I am going to be a doctor. I am going to be a big important man. Going to make you and Papa proud of me.' And I would say, 'Yes. Yes, mi son. Be a doctor for yu Mamie and Papa.' I would sit up night after night with him beating the books there till he pass the scholarship to school. I was proud that I had such a serious boy. Never grinny-grinny like those other children around. Walk and hold himself straight from those days. Like a little soldier."

"Lawd, woman, is foreign mad him," Grampa would finally snap out, goaded beyond endurance into speech. "What you want to go into all them old-time story for? What is past is past. The boy leave here good-good as you full well know. Don't is the two of we did walk with him to Number Two pier and watch him board the ship? The SS *Caroni.* I will never forget the day. We send off a good-good boy to England dress in him suit and tie, looking like a little Englishman before him even reach. Is them place there mash him up. People not suppose to go so far from home. It weaken yu constitution. You nuh see how much people round here gone mad from foreign?"

What Grampa said made me think. I started to think of all the people we knew who had gone away and come back. And several that I could think of were what we would call "not righted." Miss Pringle's daughter Gloria came back from the States talking to herself, acting like mad-ants all day long until she went right off her head. And then there was Bagman, who was somebody's pickney as he often told us, though everyone had forgotten whose. Bagman dressed in crocus-bag clothes black and stiff with dirt and he slept on the pavement outside Chin's hardware shop and didn't trouble a soul unless it was full moon, which is when he went into the banana field behind the shop and brayed like a donkey. Bagman had gone to England to fight in the war and that's how he came back. Mr. Robinson had a son in Bellevue who had also gone to England to study and Miss Lor's daughter had killed herself and her two babies there after her husband left her for another lady. Was there something in the atmosphere of foreign, I wondered then, that made people go mad, as Grampa was suggesting?

At the time I was very interested because I wanted to go away myself, wanted to go to England to study when I got big and graduated from high school. But I had no intention of going mad though I could see myself learning to speak rich and fruity like Uncle. That was what I liked best about him. But I was also sorry for him: I truly wanted to know what had happened to make him act the way he did. I used to imagine from the way he walked that he was holding all his pain in, that if he could only talk about it, spill it all, his body would relax again. But Uncle never talked. And, after a while, nobody talked to Uncle. Well, Grampa wasn't given to talking anyway, though when Uncle first came, he tried. But increasingly as Grampa realized that Uncle was mad, you could see him drawing up everything inside himself, the same way Uncle had done, for Grampa was ashamed. He was ashamed because Uncle wasn't keeping his madness at home. He would have felt better, he told Gran one night, if Uncle had the kind of madness that you could lock up, so nobody would know about it. But we couldn't keep Uncle off the road, and he went parading his madness every day for all the world to see.

After a while, everyone in the district accepted that Uncle was mad. They stopped calling him "Mister Sonny" and "Doctor" and "Sir," which they'd called him when he first came. Now he was plain "Sonny" to everyone, including the little children who would trail behind him mimicking his stiff-legged gait, his fixed smile. The adults were more tolerant, though they shouted out things good-humouredly as he passed. Then he became such a fixture that they no longer noticed him. After a few months Uncle became a local "character," like Bagman or Turnfoot Tiny.

Grampa's drinking buddies in the bar no longer referred to Uncle at all in Grampa's presence. They behaved as if the son he had talked about for twenty years had suddenly vanished from the face of the earth. Grampa was relieved that nobody talked about Uncle, but at the same time he felt ashamed; cheated and ashamed. Anything would be preferable to having a child afflicted with madness.

Gran and Grampa became fearful for me. Aside from showing her nervousness about my studying too much, Gran would say, "Girlie, dear, when you go away to high school you must never ever tell anybody that you have a mad uncle. Never. For they might think you tar with the same brush, you know. Madness can run in the family. Don't ever let anybody know your uncle mad."

I was glad when I got the scholarship that would take me away to boarding school, for having Uncle around in the district was hard enough. I had to put up with so much teasing from the children at school, had got into the first and only fist fights of my life because of Uncle. I was glad I was going far away from the problem.

By that time, too, I have to confess, I had begun to resent having Uncle around. When it had been just me and Gran and Grampa, we seemed to fit together so well. Now with Uncle there we all sat at mealtimes totally silent, nobody saying a word, the three of us pretending he wasn't there, but totally conscious of him nonetheless. He would delicately cut up his food and only go through the motion of eating. I sometimes wondered how he stayed alive. And always the three-piece suit, which was getting more ragged and dirty every day, the stiff posture, the fixed smile. Gran and Grampa became as distant and silent as Uncle was, and soon the house, which had once seemed to be so warm, so full of love and caring, now seemed empty and cold, as if nobody lived there anymore.

Every time I went back home on holidays the house seemed emptier, the two old people and Uncle appeared to rattle around in it like dried peas in a pod, all shrinking in their separate spaces, deadlocked in their silences. Then, during one vacation, a few years after Uncle returned, something did happen. As I ran into the house one day, I could see Uncle's head peeping out of the half-open door of his room. He had evidently been looking out for me for, as soon as he saw me, he put his finger to his lips and beckoned me into his room. He closed the door behind me, still cautioning me to silence with one hand while from the other he dangled a key. I had no time to think what the key might unlock for he went straight to his trunk, which was sitting under his bed, pulled it out, lifted it onto the bed, and inserted the key into the lock. At last I was going to see what was in the mysterious trunk. Over the years Gran and Grampa had speculated endlessly on what he could be keeping inside it, having never given up hope that it might contain some treasure, such as the foreign goods for which they so longed.

But when Uncle turned the key and flung open the trunk, I saw that all he had inside it were papers: letters in envelopes going brown and brittle with age, the letters so creased from handling they fell apart as he touched them; hundreds of sheets of yellowing paper covered with what I took to be Uncle's tiny and precise handwriting. As he took all the papers out and lay them on the table, he talked nonstop, never giving me a chance to look at anything, for as soon as he had emptied the trunk, he immediately started putting everything back in.

"Here, Girlie, here are all my letters to the Queen," he said, waving packages of paper at me. "And here are her replies. But this, Girlie," he said, grabbing up a fistful of sheets, "this is my case. My case that I have been preparing for years now, all my life. Six million pounds in damages I am claiming. Don't you think I am owed compensation? I and my children and my children's children? I never wanted to go into that hospital, Girlie. They dragged me in there. Kidnapped me, you have to say. Inflicted indignity and disfigurement on my person. Took out my heart and put in a mechanical one. And you know why, Girlie?" Uncle thrust his face at me and for once his eyes seemed to focus as they bored into mine.

"No, Uncle," I said.

"Because those people only understand machines. That's what I found out about them. Want to turn us all into machines. So they can work us as they like and wear us down as they like and nobody can say one little thing. Because we are not human any more. But see here, Girlie, I am making my case. I want you to take it for me. Take it to England. Take it to the Queen. You can tell her I am sorry, if you want. Tell the Queen I'm sorry to discombobulate her. But it's a long time now I've been waiting for my settlement. And I can't wait any more."

Uncle continued putting the papers back into the trunk and, as soon as he finished, he locked it, looked at his watch, and announced that it was time for him to go for his walk. As far as I knew, he never opened his trunk to show anyone his papers again, and, as he had done, I locked the secret up in my heart.

I eventually left the problem behind as I had once prayed to do; I finished school and won the scholarship I had worked so hard for to go to university in England. Gran wept over me as I packed to leave, for in her joy at my success she never failed to point out that I was leaving to study medicine, too, just as Uncle had done. "Do, Girlie, take care of yourself. Don't study too hard, you hear. Don't mek what happen to poor Sonny happen to you. Is studiration bring him to this."

From England, I wrote nothing but good news to Gran, but I fretted and prayed for my own sanity, for at times I caught a glimpse of what might have happened to Uncle. I never tried to get in touch with Uncle's family there, for what would I have had to say to them?

There were many times during the next ten years that I desperately wanted to go home, but of course I could never have afforded it. First Grampa falling ill and dying, then the news of Gran's own brief illness followed almost immediately by the telegram telling me of her death. I was glad that I had my studies to keep my grief in check, and I tried hard not to focus on the fact that I was now alone in the world – except for Uncle. I worried constantly about Uncle, who, of course, never replied to my letters, but I got news from time to time from the neighbours who kept an eye on him. Nothing seemed to have changed in his life.

As soon as I qualified and returned home, I headed for the

country to look for Uncle, not even bothering to warn him of my arrival. As I neared the house, I braced myself for the worst, but I was surprised to find when I got there that, in some subtle and undefined way, the house no longer seemed as empty and cold as it had been when I left. I was astonished that Uncle knew exactly who I was as soon as he opened the door; perhaps he still saw me as his little sister. I noticed that he had changed in superficial ways: he no longer wore the suit – perhaps it had simply fallen apart – but he was still dressed formally enough, for with his short-sleeved shirt he wore suspenders and a tie. Before he died, Grampa had given the neighbour permission to farm the land, on condition that they looked after Uncle. All they did was put food in front of him and wash his clothes, but he didn't seem to need anything else. Uncle still appeared oblivious to everything around him, still wore on his face that secret inward-turning smile. He still held himself stiff as a wind-up toy and, I discovered, still went for walks at four in the afternoon regular as clockwork, swinging his cane and lifting what was now a soft felt hat to everyone he passed.

Inside, the house looked as though it hadn't been dusted for years. I saw at once that Uncle had at last opened the trunk, for he had spread out his papers over every flat surface. Floor, beds, tables, chairs were covered with his papers – letters, envelopes, and the loose sheets with the minuscule, precise handwriting.

"Girlie," he said in greeting, "it is almost ready. I have almost finished my case. I am getting ready to send it to the Queen."

I looked around, half expecting the ghostly presence of Gran and Grampa to materialize, but, for the first time since they'd died, it sank in that I would never see them again. As I stood there I was overcome with the feeling that despite its neglect and its strange devolution, the house itself no longer felt dry and rattling as it had when I'd left. It felt light and airy now, as if it had shed its burdens of age and secrets and solitudes. I looked at Uncle, who was so thin he appeared almost weight-less. As he moved around the room, talking, lifting letters from fragmenting envelopes, putting them back again, gesturing in that old mechanical way, it seemed to me that behind the remote smile, behind the stiff soldierly posture, a heart seemed to be beating steadily. It was as if when he finally found room to open the trunk and spread out his papers, he had, for the first time in his life, poured out his presence.

Window

Four months after Jesse left for Kingston to find a husband, Ma Lou's grandson Devonshire came home from Colón. Strutted in, was more like it. He arrived in full-blown Colón style – a brown draped suit, complete with watch chain with dangling charms and a fat gold watch inside his fob pocket, matching brown derby, yellow boots, and a walking-stick with the head of a wolf carved in ivory on the handle. "Dev, what a sweet-man you turn into," Mama laughed when, trailing the sweet smell of brilliantine, he came into the bedroom to pay his respects to her the minute he arrived. It was the first time in years Brid had heard her mother laugh.

Dev didn't see Brid when he came, for she shot out of sight as soon as she saw him approaching across the yard, but she had a good look at him; Brid was good at seeing through cracks in walls and half-pulled shutters, from behind closed doors and between floorboards. But Brid didn't like to be seen.

"How's Jesse?" she heard Dev ask Mama. "And little Bridget?"

"Jesse is gone away, my dear, gone to Kingston to stay with her Aunt Irene. Four months now she's gone and left us. Brid is still around, though you won't believe it's her when you see her, Dev. Just me and Brid left. And Ma Lou."

"Brid," her mother called in her weak, pale voice. "Bridget. Come Brid and look who's here."

"Brid-get!" Ma Lou yelled in her loud marketwoman's voice.

But Brid, who was peering through a crack into Mama's room, didn't answer. She held her breath so they wouldn't hear her and marvelled at Dev. How handsome he had become. He had grown almost a foot taller in the five years he was gone, and had filled out. Looked like a real grown-up man. Dev was hardly much older than she was now when he left home. A real langillala skinny-foot boy he was. And look at him now. Brid was pleased to see him, for he'd been the closest thing she had to a brother. In the past she could always rely on him to play games with her, pick mangoes from the tallest branches, or knock down the ripe soursops. He would dry her tears when she cried and frighten her with tales of duppies and Blackartman. But she wouldn't come out and talk to him because she was dismayed to see the old Dev vanished and this impressive, self-assured stranger in his place. It was as if Dev too had let her down. His coming, instead of making her feel happy as she had imagined, just made her feel more ashamed. Ashamed of herself, her unfashionable hair and hand-me-down clothes, ashamed of the old house with the rotting verandah and falling shingles and peeling woodwork, ashamed of her mother who was perpetually ill, the smell of the sick-room, damp, and decay, ashamed of their poverty and their pride. Or rather, Mama's and Jesse's pride, for she had none, or so they told her.

Ma Lou wasn't too impressed by Dev – she didn't want a sweet-man for a grandson. She felt better when after a few weeks of his walking up and down the whole district to show off his clothes, his Panama strut, his American accent, and his Panama gold rings – like all the other young men who came back from foreign – Dev took off his good clothes and his jewellery, put on a pair of American denim overalls and one of his old shirts, and went into the garden with his machete. Now *that* Ma Lou could understand, for fly high, fly low, she said after Dev left to get work on building the Panama Canal, there was nothing to beat working on the land. But Dev didn't really go into the garden to work; he just wanted to get into the feel of things again, to rid himself of the dust and the sound of dynamite blasting in his ears, the American straw boss yelling, trains shunting and the interminable rain, and the smell of damp clothes and mildew and dead things rotting in the streets.

"Dev looking for land to buy," Ma Lou confided to Mama, as she sponged her body down and turned her in the bed. "Want to put him money into land. And house. That Dev have him head well screw on," she said with satisfaction, as if she had done the screwing, for she believed that whatever sense Dev showed in managing his affairs it was she who had beaten it into him. Dev's mother had come and placed him in her arms shortly after he was born and was never heard from again. Dev's father, Ma Lou's son, died soon after, when a tree he was chopping down fell the wrong way. So she had ended up with Dev for her very own.

"Maybe he could buy ours," Mama said and laughed again, but Brid listening on the other side of the wall knew it wasn't a genuine laugh like the one she had greeted Dev with. This was the laugh of bitterness, for Brid knew it pained her mother to see what she and her family had come to, while people like Dev, whom they would never have counted in the old days, were now moving up in the world. Brid knew because it was all her mother used to talk about to Jesse.

Brid couldn't understand how Mama and Jesse could be so proud of their white skin when so far as she could see there were no advantages to be derived from it. At school, it is true, the big girls would sit with their backs against the buttresses of the church (the school was in the same yard) and during recess take turns combing and plaiting her hair, praising her to the skies for how beautiful it was and how wonderful it was to have good, tall hair. But then during class the boys sitting behind would thread her long plait through the hole for the inkwell in their desk and tie it into a knot. So clever were they that sometimes she wouldn't even realize what was happening until the bell rang and she stood up and pulled the desk over, sending ink pots and slates flying while the bad boys dashed out of the schoolroom yelling with laughter and the other children shouted at her as she cried with frustration trying to free herself from the desk. So what good was that? She saw no advantage to having fair skin because everyone around her was black and she stood out, and she didn't want to stand out, didn't want them to notice her, because then they would notice her poverty, her house falling down, her bedridden mother. Everyone else around was poor, too, ate turn cornmeal and shad just like them, or worse, had houses ten times worse than theirs, without floors even, and had no nice furniture like they had – the pieces that hadn't yet been sold. But that was different. "Black people born to be poor," Mama had said. "Nobody expects any better of them."

"So why were we born poor?" Brid asked Jesse in their room that night.

"We weren't born poor," Jesse said. "We're only poor because Papa ran away and left us and there was nobody to look after the place. Mama got sick and everything."

Brid knew this by heart; she had heard it many times before. So why didn't they just accept their lot in life, she asked, and stop behaving as if they were better than everybody else?

"Bridget, you'll understand when you're older," Jesse said. "God gave you beautiful skin and long lovely hair and you should thank him for it and take care of it. Some day a man will come along who will appreciate those things and you'll be glad then that you don't have ol'nayga skin and picky-picky hair."

That's all Jesse lived for: for a man to come along. Meanwhile, she took good care of herself; rubbed cocoa butter into her skin every single night and brushed her hair a hundred times morning and evening. She used chewstick to clean her teeth every time she ate, rubbed anatto into her lips and cheeks and put charcoal on her lashes, washed her hair with aloe and rinsed it with rosemary, tried out a new hairstyle every day, twisting her head this way and that to see the effect in the tarnished three-way vanity mirror, though nobody ever saw her except Brid and Mama and Ma Lou.

When Jesse was twenty, she and Mama and Ma Lou realized that nobody would ever come along to notice her where they lived, since nobody ever came at all, so she was sent to Aunt Irene in Kingston.

Brid liked it when Jesse was around because then nobody made any demands on her. Jesse was the one who helped Ma Lou with Mama in the sick-room, who went and spent her time talking and reading to her. Brid hated going into the room, hated the smell, the way her mother looked, her querulous complaints. She never went in if she could help it. Now that she had finished elementary school, with no money to send her further, she preferred to spend her time helping Ma Lou in the garden or the kitchen, places where Jesse hated to be.

When Dev left, there was no man to help them, except for Marse Ron, who came to do the hard work as needed, like digging the yam hills and helping to plant and stake the yams, doing the ploughing and cutting and burning. Marse Ron was hired to do these things when there was money, or for a share of the crop, when there was none. When the land was cleared, Brid went out and helped Ma Lou with the planting, or reaping the cocoa, picking the coffee, peeling the ginger, or shelling the corn.

It was Ma Lou who arranged for her friend Miss Gertie, who was still selling in the market, to come and buy their crops. Without Ma Lou, Brid thought, they'd be nothing. Ma Lou had lived in a little cottage at the back which Dev shared with her until he went away. Then she came and lay down her bedding in the room beside Mama's and slept there every night. Ma Lou was born in the cottage because her parents used to work with Mama's grandparents, and even after her parents died, Ma Lou just stayed on. When Mama was born, it was Ma Lou who looked after her, and then she looked after Mama's babies. Ma Lou had been with them all her life; it was unthinkable that she should not be there always. Ma Lou belonged to them as they belonged to her. Brid used to think that their lives and Ma Lou's were intertwined like the Scotchman fig which grew on to the big silk-cotton tree, twisting and embedding itself into the trunk of the other to such an extent that it was hard to figure out which was the silk-cotton and which the fig. It was Ma Lou who made all the decisions now about the family, she who planted the crops and sold what needed to be sold to earn them a little cash, she who went to market to buy; it was she who fed them and looked after them, for Mama was now helpless as a child. Brid never understood what was wrong with Mama; she only knew she had taken to her bed after Papa left (which she was too young to remember) and hadn't ever left her room again.

When Jesse went off to Kingston she promised to write, but it was three months now since they'd heard from her. In her first letters Jesse had told of the grand reception she'd had from Aunt Irene and Uncle Cyrus and her cousins, about her new wardrobe, her new life. But then the letters ceased. Mama had since heard from Aunt Irene, heard that Jesse was getting on and had fitted into the family, that they expected great things of her. But Jesse didn't write again.

Brid could just imagine Jesse in her new wardrobe, with a fashionable hairdo, charming all the young men who came to call, having a hard time making up her mind, choosing which one to marry. Jesse had promised that as soon as she settled down, she would send for Brid, send her clothes to travel in, proper shoes, and a suitcase. Promised to find Brid a husband, too, though this made Brid laugh because she was sixteen and she couldn't imagine anyone liking her, much less wanting to marry her. Now Brid cried herself to sleep because there was no one to laugh with.

Dev never even saw Brid until he had been back for a few weeks: he had been so busy walking up and down showing off, and when he came back to the cottage at night, they would all have gone to bed. It was only after he decided that he had been seen by everyone he had wanted to see him, and had put his good clothes away and stopped walking about, that he saw Brid in the garden one day. She was in the garden helping Ma Lou stake tomatoes, with her thick black hair in one long plait down her back, and her skirt pulled up at the waist to show her bare legs, just like Ma Lou. But as soon as she looked up and saw him, she fled into the house. She never came back and he helped his grandmother finish the job. He had been astonished to see her, to see that she was no longer the skinny little girl he had left behind, had turned into a fine young lady, better looking, he thought with satisfaction, than that Jesse who, even when they were small, was so full of airs and graces and who would never have gone into the yard without stockings, no matter how patched they were, and who would never pull up her skirt at the waist to show her legs.

"Brid turn into a fine young lady," he said to his grandmother.

"Yes, but God alone know what is going to become of that child. I never worry about Jesse. Jesse will get by. But that Brid. Not a one to mind her. And she wild like mongoose. What going happen to Brid?"

Brid never spoke to Dev at all, she was too shy, felt he had risen too far above her now, so she always managed to disappear when she saw him coming. Then she would rush to peek at him from behind the slatted shutters in the bedroom. She really wished she could talk to Dev; she wanted to find out all about his adventures, what had happened to him in the years he had been away, but she had to be content with the second-hand accounts she got from Ma Lou or listen through the wall when he came to talk to Mama.

Dev was disappointed that Brid no longer wanted to be his friend, to talk to him. Now he was back home, he felt restless and at loose ends, didn't know what to do with himself. He wanted to make something of his life, buy land, build a proper house for himself and his grandmother, for he was now a master carpenter, wanted to go into the house-building business. He could make it, he felt sure, for he had been taught by the Americans and nobody could beat them when it came to modern, efficient ways. The country was ripe for people like him, he knew. He was looking for land, yes, for a property, had money to burn, so he didn't know why he was still hanging around this yard like an angry bull tied to a post. He had been shocked to come home, to see the house with one side almost fallen in, to see the squalor in which they lived. He'd completely forgotten what it had been like. Only the land was as he remembered it: the hazy blue mountains in the distance, the greenness of everything, the freshness of the air, the brightness of the stars at night. He took it all as a benediction, after the hell of Culebra, of Colón.

He couldn't sleep and took to walking outside at night, to look at the stars, to feel the cool air, and for a long time wasn't even conscious that he always ended up standing in the darkness of the cocoa walk staring at the shutters of Bridget's room. Brid saw him, though, for she hardly slept either, and one night she had seen his shadow move in the cocoa walk, saw him standing there looking at her window. After that, she peeked through the shutters every night, stood by the window for hours, until she saw him. Didn't know why it gave her such unimaginable joy to see him standing there, looking at her window, to stand there and watch him. Only when his shadow disappeared would she get back into bed and, feeling deeply secure, sleep soundly for the rest of the night.

The idea took a long time to crystallize in Dev's mind, but when it did, it all seemed so right to him. He was now ready to take a wife, why shouldn't he marry Brid? What was the use of building a house if he didn't have a woman? Why shouldn't he buy this house and land from them, so they could all continue to live together, for how could he separate his grandmother from Brid and her mother? Weren't they all one family? He turned his carpenter's eyes on the house, walked around and assessed it carefully, admiring its proportions, and came to the conclusion that the structure, built of the finest mahogany and cedar, was sound enough. It was not too far gone that it couldn't be restored. He would need to add bathrooms with modern plumbing and a proper kitchen. The verandah could be enlarged. If they hadn't sold any of the land in his absence, he knew it was some two hundred acres of reasonably good soil, just about what he was looking for. He would have to have a proper survey done, get an outsider to fix the price; he would never want anyone to say he had taken advantage of Brid and her mother. When he had thought it all through, he broke the news to his grandmother.

Instead of being overjoyed as he had thought she would be at this solution to their problems, for she spent all her time worrying about Brid's future, his grandmother nearly fainted; she had been so shocked she sat down heavily on the bed in the cottage where he was talking to her.

"You? Marry Bridget?" she said. "Dev, you gone crazy or what?"

"What you mean?" he asked, genuinely confused.

"Dev, you know oil and water don't mix from morning. You go away is true and do well for yourself. I am proud of you. No woman could be prouder of her son and that is the Lord's own truth. But that still don't give you no right to think you can marry white people daughter. Don't even bother to think of it. You want kill off Miss Carmen?"

"Well, somebody has to marry Brid, and what is wrong with me? You mean them old-time something don't break down yet? Look at Brid and Miss Carmen, poor as church-mouse. You'd think they'd be glad to have somebody that could take care of them."

"You see that now. You come in just like all them Colón man there. And I did think you have a little more sense in yu head. Go to Colón and make a little money and you all come back same way – thinking you just as good as everybody else. Wanting to change the whole world overnight. Out to create nothing but bad blood and confusion."

"Gran, what confusion you see me creating?" Dev protested. "Why you so unfair? You behaving as if is something criminal I proposing."

But his grandmother refused to listen to him anymore, threw her apron over her head and cried the living eye-water for his boldness. He had never seen his grandmother cry before except the time Mr. Jasper went away, and he was so shattered that he put on his hat and left, went down to the village and drank rum, and came home late and went straight to bed. Next day he took some of his clothes and went to stay with a Colón mate who lived not far away. But even as he laughed and talked with his *paseiro*, he couldn't control his thoughts, began to wonder if he did right in coming back and if he should stay in this country at all, feeling that while he had gone away and been changed so much, nothing here had changed.

They had all wanted to come back home so badly, if they could survive blackwater and yellow fever, typhoid and malaria, the dynamite blasts and the train accidents, the snake-bites and the floods and overwork, didn't end up in the asylum or in jail, and if they ever managed to save enough money or win the lottery. Nobody wanted to live with Jim Crow on the American Canal Zone. But until you saved enough, you put up with it and swallowed your pride, accepted that you were "silver," not "gold," as the races were categorized – and paid, got into the habit of averting your eyes when the white American women walked by and smiling when they addressed you as "Boy," got used to saying, "yassuh," "nosuh," to everything their white husbands said, for they controlled your lives. You did the same as the Negroes from the States did. But the islanders knew that those men didn't know any better, it came as natural to them as eating and sleeping to behave in this sub-servient manner, and they viewed them with scorn. *They* didn't have a home to go back to where the climate was natural, instead of this endless rain, and where you were a subject of the King of England. A British subject. Good as any man. Equal to any man before the law. British law.

Dev had to laugh now at how naive they all were, how silly in their belief that they were better off in their own country; for it wasn't their country at all. It was a country just like the Canal Zone where the white man reigned supreme, and where people like him were expected to remain their semi-slaves and servants. Yassuh. Nosuh. Only there were no signs which said "Silver" and "Gold." Here, they were simply expected to recognize the invisible signs, to be born knowing their place. Dev thought wryly that with the opening of the Panama

Canal, to which so many black men had given their life's blood, the Americans could see nothing incongruous about the motto they had chosen for their grand enterprise and cut in stone on their administrative building: "The Land Divided: The World United." But, he reflected, the world was united only to further the purpose of white commerce. On other matters which hinged on the colour of a man's skin, the world would stay forever divided.

Yet while Dev could see the divisions in wider terms, nearer home he found it difficult to accept this cynical philosophy. Was his grandmother so right after all? For hadn't he played with Brid and Jesse from when they were children, grown up with them like a brother? Granted that, long before he left home, Jesse had ceased to have anything to do with him, but he never bothered much with Jesse anyway, she was always too full of herself. But Brid, now, hadn't she always been his little sister? The Jaspers were the only white people around, and because they were so much a part of his life, he had never really remarked on the difference in their colour. He was aware he was different because he and his grannie lived on the Jaspers' land, had no land of their own, were the Jaspers' servants, which is why they lived in a separate cottage instead of in the big house. But the Jaspers had come down in the world, his grannie was always saying, and after a while they were all poor together. Cooked together and ate together. Up to when he went away, sixteen and very young and foolish, he thought that poverty conferred equality.

Dev stayed with his friend for a while, thinking things through, and then he decided to go away again, perhaps to

Costa Rica or Cuba this time, or even to the United States itself; at least you knew where you stood with the Americans. There was nothing for him here. But he couldn't get Brid out of his mind, her startled face as she looked up from staking tomatoes and saw him, her sun-browned legs flashing and her long plait swinging as she dashed into the house. More and more he wondered if Brid had stayed away from him only because she was shy or "wild" as his grandmother called her. Or had she become like Jesse now that she was grown up, seeing him only as black to her white? Was that why she didn't want to speak to him? He decided that he was going, yes, but first he had to know, had to call to Brid and make her look at him at least. Even if she never said a word, if she looked at him, he would read her like a book.

When Dev went off to stay with his friend, Brid had ceased to sleep at nights, stood by the window waiting for him till dawn. Cried the whole night through. Would he ever come back? Why did she feel so alone again now he was no longer there? She felt more bereft even than when Jesse had left her. Dev and his grandmother had had a quarrel, that much she knew, but what was the cause she could never find out, no matter how hard she listened. "Dev go way and come back too full of himself, ya," was all she heard Ma Lou say to her mother when Mama asked what had happened to him. So that didn't tell her much about where Dev had gone and when he would be back. And she had been so mean to him. Dev was her friend and she hadn't even bothered to speak to him; he probably thought she was a snob like Jesse. If Dev ever came back, she promised herself, no matter how difficult she found it, she would force herself to go and speak to him, let him know she was glad to have him back, let him know – but she was afraid to admit anything else, even to herself.

Dev came back and told Ma Lou he was going away again, and he couldn't bear the look in her eyes. She said nothing but she went around singing mournful hymns all day, even after he told her that he would spend some money to fix up the Jaspers' house so she and Miss Carmen and Bridget would at least have a solid roof over their heads. He made sure to tell her he was doing it for her, since he knew she would never leave there until her dying day. When she told Miss Carmen that Dev was going to fix the roof and the floors (without telling her the last part), Miss Carmen said, "God bless Dev, he was always a good boy," and turned her face to the wall and sighed.

In a matter of days, Dev measured up everything, arranged to buy the shingles and lumber and nails and get a few of his old Colón mates to come and help him once the lumber arrived. He wasn't going to do the extensive refurbishing he had envisaged, just enough to keep the three women dry and prevent them falling through the rotten floorboards.

He was so busy arranging all this that he gave no thought to Brid for the first few days after he came back. It was only when all the arrangements had been made and he was waiting for his mates to come that he started to go outside again at night, and though he did not intend it, his feet invariably led him to the cocoa walk facing Brid's room. He remembered his decision to confront her, to force her to give him some sign of how she felt, whether she too saw this unbridgeable chasm between them, but he wasn't sure how he was going to achieve this. He hoped that all the excitement of the next few weeks, the hammering and the sawing, might draw her out of her shell.

Now he stood dumbly looking at her room, wondering why he felt so unbearably sad, until the cold night air drove him inside.

The first night he returned, Brid had seen him, for she had been looking every night. He stood in the shadows of the cocoa walk but she knew he was there and she found it hard to control her heartbeats. The minute she'd seen him she had wanted to throw open her shutters to let him know she was there. But though her hand reached countless times for the latch, she couldn't bring herself to open it. Then he was gone and she climbed into bed no longer feeling consoled by his presence but overwhelmed by her cowardice. Every night it was the same; she would reach for the latch, willing herself to open it, but could never find the courage to carry the action through.

She dragged herself sorrowfully through each day, Ma Lou for once taking no notice since by now she was frantically having to look after the needs of the men who had come to work on the house as well as Mama's. Brid helped her out in the kitchen, glad to be kept busy all day long. She stayed out of sight though, hearing rather than seeing the men hammering away at shingles, window frames and floorboards. Soon they would be done, she knew, and she wondered if Dev would go with them when they left. She desperately wanted him to stay, knowing he still gazed at her window every night.

One day, Ma Lou dolefully announced that Dev thought the

work would be finished in another week and he planned to leave then with his mates. Perhaps it was the alarming finality of the news that galvanized Brid, for that night in her room, instead of staring at her window and condemning herself for her cowardice, she forced herself to imagine the very actions she was so afraid to carry through. To her surprise, she found that she could actually envision herself getting off the bed, walking to the window and, with a sense of wonder at her boldness, throwing open the shutters.

You Think I Mad, Miss?

You think I mad, Miss? You see me here with my full head of hair and my notebook and pencil, never go out a street without my stockings straight and shoes shine good for is so my mother did grow me. Beg you a smalls, nuh? Then why your face mek up so? Don't I look like somebody pickney? Don't I look like teacher? Say what? Say why I living on street then? Then is who tell you I living on street? See here, is Sheraton I live. All them box and carochies there on the roadside? Well, I have to whisper and tell you this for I don't want the breeze to catch it. You see the wappen-bappen on the streetside there? Is one old lady ask me to watch it for her till she come back. And cause mi heart so good, me say yes. I watching it day and night though is Sheraton I live. For the old lady don't come back yet. Quick before the light change for I don't eat nutten from morning. I don't know is what sweet you so. But thank you all the same. Drive good, you hear.

I hope you don't hear already, Sar, what that foolish Doctor Bartholomew saying about me all over town? Is him should lock up in Bellevue and all the people inside there set free, you know. But he couldn't keep me lock up for I smarter than all of them. That's what Teacher used to tell me. I come brighter than all the other pickney around. And tree never grow in my face neither. Beg you a little food money there nuh before the light turn green. A who you calling dutty? A why you a wind up yu window and mek up yu face? You know say is Isabella Francina Myrtella Jones this you a talk to? And since when dutty bwoy like you think you can eggs-up so talk to Miss Catherine daughter that studying to turn teacher? Why you a turn yu head a gwan seh you no see me? I know you see me all right for, though I don't behave as if I notice, I know all you young men sitting on the bridge every day there eyeing me as I pass. Would like to drag me down, drag me right down to your level. Have my name outa road like how you all have Cane-piece Icilda. And that is why I hold up my head and wear two slip under my skirt. And I don't pay you all no mind. For what I would want with any of you? Then wait, you not even giving me a two cents there and I don't eat from morning? Gwan, you ol' red nayga you. From I see you drive up I shoulda know seh is that Bartholomew send you. Send you to torment me. You ugly just like him, to rah. Go weh!

⌐ ⌐

Hello, my sweet little darling. What you have to give me today? I don't eat a thing from morning, Mother. I wouldn't tell you

lie in front of your little girl. Is same so my little one did look,
you know? Seven pound, six and a half ounce she did weigh,
and pretty like a picture. Is bad-minded people make them take
her away. Thank you, Mother. God bless you and the little darling. Say who take her? Well me have to whisper it for me don't
want the breeze to catch it. But is that Elfraida Campbell, that's
who. The one that did say me did grudge her Jimmy Watson.
Then you nuh remember her? Is she and her mother burn bad
candle for me mek me buck mi foot and fall. For I never had
those intentions. No such intentions. Is two slip I wear under
my skirt for I was studying to be teacher. Is Miss Catherine my
mother, you know. Say the light changing? You gone? God
bless you, my precious daughter.

— —

Young girl, I see you courting. But don't mek that young man
behind steering wheel have business with you before you married, you hear? For once he know you he drag you down, drag
you down to nutten. Then is pure ashes you eat. Pure dutty fe
yu bed. The two of you a laugh! You better mind is nuh laugh
today, cry tomorrow. But what a way you resemble Jimmy
Watson ee? Him was handsome just like you. Thank you, mi
darling, the two of you drive good, you hear. Say who is Jimmy
Watson? Then you never know him? The same Jimmy Watson
that did come as the assistant teacher and all the girls did love
him off. Well, not me. For I didn't have no intention to take on
young man before I get certification. Is Shortwood Teacher
Training College I was going to, you know. Eh-eh, then you

just wind up yu window and drive off so? What a bad-mannered set of children ee!

— ~ —

Like I was saying, Sar, I was busy with my studying and that is why that Elfraida Campbell did get her hooks into Jimmy Watson. For what Jimmy would really want with girl that can barely sign her name, nuh matter she walk and fling her hips about? So I just study and bide my time. Oh, God bless you, Sar, I could kiss yu hand. Is from morning I don't eat, you know. But that Elfraida is such a wicked girl, Sar, she and her mammy. If you ever see her, please call the constable for me, for is plenty things she have to answer for. Courthouse business, Sar. If she and her mammy didn't work negromancy on me, Doctor Bartholomew wouldn't be looking for me all now. But he will never never find me. You want to know why? You see that big box there a roadside? Is there I hide, you know. Once I get inside my box, not a living soul can find me. They could send out one million policeman to search for me. Two million soldier. The whole of Salvation Army. They could look into the box till they turn fool. They could shine they torch, bring searchlight and X-ray and TV and atomic bomb. Not one of them could ever find me. Aright, Sar. You gone? God bless you.

— ~ —

Look at my darling lady in the white car who always give me something. God bless you and keep you, my dear. Mine how you travel, you hear? Satan set plenty snares in the world for the innocent. Take me, now. Is not me did go after Jimmy Watson. As God is mi judge. Him and Elfraida Campbell was getting on good-good there. It was a disgrace that a girl should act so common and make people carry her name all over the district like that. Even the breeze did tek it. And he was man of education too. What about his reputation? So when he first put question to me I didn't business, for I never want people have anything to say about me and I don't get my certificate yet. But it was just as I thought. Jimmy Watson wanted a woman that wouldn't shame him, a decent woman with broughtupcy and plenty book-learning. That is how he put it to me. And I resist and I resist but, after a while, that Jimmy Watson so handsome and have sweet-mout so, him confabulation just wear down mi resistance. Never mind bout certification and teacher college – eh-eh, you gone already. God bless you, sweetheart.

— ⁓ —

Sar, you see that police fellow there from morning? The constable that is like a thorn in mi side? Can't get a good night rest from him beating on mi bedroom with him stick. Is what do him ee? Is Satan send him to torment me, you know. You know who Satan is? Beg you a dollar, nuh? A hungry, you see. A don't eat a thing from morning. Satan and Bartholomew is one and the same. Then you never know? And you look so bright? Look as if is university you come from. Don't is so? Well, thank you, Sar. The good Lord will bless you. And if you see Bartholomew there up at U.C., tell him is lie. Is lie he telling about the baby. Say it was all in mi mind. You ever hear a piece of madness like that? Is Bartholomew they suppose to lock up and the child weigh eight and three-quarter pound? A spanking baby boy. Is that cause Elfraida Campbell to burn bad candle for me. Jealousy just drive her crazy. Eh-hm. Drive good, ya. And beg you tell government what Bartholomew going on with, you hear?

— ~ —

From I born and grow I never know man could lie like that Jimmy Watson. Is only Bartholomew lie good like him, you know, my lady and gentleman. Thank you for a smalls, Sar, for a cup of tea. Nothing pass my lips from morning. Thank you, Sar. God bless. You did know Jimmy Watson swear to my mother he never touch me? Never have a thing to do with me? Fancy that! So is who was lying with me every night there? Who was plunging into me like St. George with his sword? He cry the living eye-water the day my mother ask if he business with me, for that time the baby already on the way. I could feel it kicking inside me. And that lying Jimmy Watson say he never lay hands on me. Same thing the lying Bartholomew did tell my mother. That no man ever touch me. How man can lie so ee? So is how the baby did come then, answer me that? How baby can born so, without father? Ten and a half pound it weigh. Say what, Sar? Say why if I have children I living on street? Then is why unno red nayga so faas and facety ee? Answer me that. You see me asking you question bout fe yu pickney? Unno gwan! Think because you see me look so I don't come from nowhere? Ever see me without my paper and pencil yet? Ever see me without my shoes and stocking and two slip under my dress? Think I wear them little clingy-clingy frock without slip like that Elfraida Campbell so every man could see my backside swing when I walk? Unno gwan!

— ◆ —

So is what sweet you so, you little facety bwoy? You never see stone fling after car yet? You want me bus one in yu head? Say somebody shoulda call police? So why you don't do it, since you so shurance and force-ripe? Mek that constable bwoy come near me today. Mek them send that Bartholomew. Send for them. Do. I want them to arrest me at Lady Musgrave Road traffic light here today. I want them to take me down to court-house. I want to have my day in court. I want to stand up in front of judge and jury. I want to say "Justice" and beg him to ask them certain question. He-hey. Don't mek I laugh here today. You want to know something, sweet bwoy. Them not going to do a thing about me, you know. Say wha mek? Well, me have to whisper it, for me nuh want no breeze catch hold of it. But the reason is because they fraid. Fraid to give me my day in court. Fraid to have me ask my question there. All of them fraid. Even the judge. Even Massa God himself. For nobody want to take responsibility to answer me. Gwan, you little dutty bwoy. Yu face favour!

— —

Good day, Missis. You did say you want to hear my question? Well, beg you a money there nuh, please. I don't get a thing to eat from morning. Thank you, Miss. You want to hear my question, please? So why you winding up yu glass? Why you unmannersable so? Well, whether you want to hear or not, you stupid bitch, I, Isabella Francina Myrtella Jones, am going to tell you. So you can ease down all you want. I going to shout it from Lady Musgrave Road traffic light. I going to make the breeze take it to the four corners of everywhere. First: Is who take away my child? Second: Why Jimmy Watson lie so and say he never lie with me? Third: Why they let that Elfraida Camp-bell and her mother tie Jimmy Watson so I never even have a chance with him? Fourth: Why my mother Miss Catherine never believe anything I say again. Why she let me down so? Is obeah them obeah her too why she hand me over to that Bartholomew? Fifth: Why that Bartholomew madder than mad and he walking bout free as a bird? Who give him the right to lock up people in Bellevue and burn bright light all night and ask them all sort of foolish question? Sixth: What is the government going to do about these things? Seventh: If there is still Massa God up above, is what I do why him have to tek everybody side against me?

Swimming in the Ba'ma Grass

... SWIMMING? IN the Ba'ma grass? Who ever heard of such a thing and a big man at that? Dress in him work clothes same way, him khaki shirt and him old stain-up jeans pants and him brand new Ironman water boots that I did tell him was too big for him, this old man playing the fool in the middle of the pasture, lying there pretending he swimming with his two hands out there like he doing the crawl and his feet kicking. Look how he playing the fool till one of his boots fall off and is what that red thing like blood stain up the back of him brand new khaki shirt, is only one time it wash and look how him gone stain it up now. And is why that police boy there, the one Shannon, why he standing there with his gun in him hand and that other one there from the station, Browning, standing beside him, and the two of them watching my husband there making a fool of himself pretending he swimming? Why all the people running and shouting and Shannon waving his gun at them telling them to back-back, Shannon waving his gun at me while I run to Arnold who not swimming at all – I know he jokify but this is going too far.

You don't think the one Shannon could mad enough shoot Arnold? That is what Dorcas big boy was calling out to me when I was hanging out the clothes? Him did really say "Shannon shoot Marse Arnold"? Me not even sure now me did hear what him did say good. He was making so much noise I get confuse. He was calling my name, calling my name, "Miss Lyn, Miss Lyn. Come quick," and something about my husband and Shannon, but if he really did say Shannon shoot Arnold why me poor woman standing here thinking seh Arnold playing the fool?

See here now. Is only because I know Arnold is a man come from the sea and like to play the fool sometime; he love the sea more than anything in the whole world and when he wanted was to go to Treasure Beach and I wouldn't let him, him would lie on the floor and pretend he swimming and laugh, doing it just to annoy me, but not in a malicious way. Arnold don't have a mean bone in him body which is why everybody so vex with the way that that police boy Shannon been treating him since that time he went up to the station to complain. Trying every which way to get Arnold into trouble but he never succeed yet because everybody in this town know Arnold is a decent law-abiding man. Telling everybody, the boasy boy, say he going to get Arnold. And not a soul, not even Sarge that say him is Arnold friend, do one thing about it, because that Shannon is bull-buck-and-duppy-conqueror and everybody fraid of him. Forever boasting that he going to get

Arnold. For what? Everybody know Arnold not a complaining man. He not a quarrelling man. Look how long we live here in peace with all our neighbours. Ask any one of them. Of all the people living here, Arnold must be the only one never quarrel with nobody yet. Me really can't say the same for myself because everybody know my temper well hot. But this time it wasn't me quarrelling with anybody why Dorcas boy was making so much noise. Mark you, him was always a noisy little fellow. But what he was calling out again ee? Lawd Jesus! A can't keep a thing in mi brain.

Oh. I remember now. I was talking how my temper hot and that is why when that Shannon show impertinence to me at the police station I did fire him a box hot-hot. Me big married woman him a go put question to! A tek him big dutty nayga hand a touch me. Just because he see me there a clean up the place he must be think I one of him dutty Kingston gal. I fire him a box, you see, and him so shock, him just reel back so, and then I see some evil come into him eye, you see, and a swear to Massa God he going to kill me. But another policeman come into the room same time and Shannon turn him tail and leave. This was one of the decent fellows there – one of the Wright boys from out Christiana way – and when he ask me what happen, I tell him. And me did expect him to laugh but he look serious bout the whole thing and he say, "Miss Lyn, you have every right to box him. Facety wretch. But Shannon not a man to cross, you know. Them say is six man him kill aready in town. Is 'Enforcer' them call him there, you know. And them only send him here because town get a little too hot for him right now." Then him look round good before him whisper to me, "Is Big Man behind him, you know."

Cho! What that Wright think he playing? Everybody know bout Enforcer and which politician him kill for. But that is Kingston business. Me did hear say him was getting too big for him boots so the Big Man glad to get rid of him, send him down here to cool him off for a while. And like how no politics a go on down here, Enforcer don't have nothing to enforce.

But see here, that Shannon is a rat though, you know, a stinking dirty rat. After that, I couldn't do nothing right at the station. Shannon cross me up every time. Is like him set in wait for me. The minute I clean the floor, him would walk outside in the mud and come tramping right across it, innocent like, and I couldn't say a word. I would wash the sheets and towels and hang them on the line, and when I come back to pick them up, I find that somebody rub green bush and dutty into them. Me say, those things were so childish. If him was big and bad like they say, why him was going on like pickney so? I take the Sarge him coffee in the morning, and Sarge take one sip and swear blue light at me for somebody put salt in the sugar. Just things like that Shannon do, like pickney. But still and all he was a snake. Used to make my skin crawl. Any time I at the station and he come in, my skin just crawl. Him never trouble me again though, and I make sure to keep out of his way. But I get the feeling the whole time he looking at me and laughing inside, laughing and biding him time.

Then is what that Shannon doing standing there in the middle of the pasture in this sun hot, wearing him good Kingston shoes? Why he not at the station, eh? I never even bother to tell Arnold about him putting question to me, for you know how man stay. Even though they there quiet, them like a raging bull when they think another man even look at their woman. And then again sometimes man you would never ever consider put question to you, and your own man vex because they say is you encouragement them. So me don't say nothing. But all the little petty things Shannon doing getting on my nerves. So I start complain about the job and I tell Arnold I want to leave.

Arnold don't want me to leave for he say is the best job I ever have, cleaning up at the station and doing a little washing on the side. Arnold say is good government work and I get my pay regular, I don't have to put up with some facety woman in her kitchen and if anything should happen to him, if I stay there long enough, I will come in for a little pension.

But I fuss and fuss every day till Arnold can't stand it no longer and he ask me exactly what is happening and I still don't tell him bout Shannon. I tell him bout all the trickify things somebody doing to me and how it making my work twice as hard. I don't tell him how it burn me up day after day to go to work and see that snakey smile on Shannon face.

Well, unbeknownest to me, Arnold nuh decide to go and see the Sarge, who he know well – the two of them drinking all the time together down at One Love. But Arnold is a serious man when he ready so he don't tackle Sarge at the bar – he put on his good clothes one day and, after I leave work, he go to the station to complain to Sarge that one of the policeman have it in for me. So Sarge say he will look into it. Now, I don't know if Sarge did know what was happening – maybe Wright did tell him. Anyway, next day I go to work and he call me in and ask me how come something happening at the station and I don't tell him, look how long I work there and is my husband have to come in and lodge complaint. So then I explain to him what happen with Shannon and me and why I don't want to discuss it with Arnold. So he say "A-oh." And that is the last I hear of it.

Is the same fellow Wright did tell me how Sarge call in the Shannon there and chastise him for his treatment of me. But you see how life stay? Shannon get it into him head that is my husband that did lodge complaint to Sarge about him. And that is how the bad blood between my husband and Shannon start.

And is me cause it O God is me responsible for everything that happen in my husband life from he meet me. Is me cause him to be living here, working on the land, something he never want to do for he really wanted was to live by the sea. Is there him come from, down Treasure Beach way, is a hard set of people living down there, you know. If them not fighting with the sea them fighting the land, for it hardly ever rain and it hardly have any proper tree or no little green grass. Is Mandeville I come from, up in the hill where it green and cool all the time and me not lying at all, me just never like the part of the world that Arnold come from. It never look natural to me, the way place suppose to look, and the people them don't look natural neither. And I never never could stand the sea.

Is how me did get on to meeting Arnold? Me can't even remember, I tell you, mi brain gone.

Arnold used to deal with my Daddy, that time when I was a young girl and my Daddy did have a dray. He used to go down to Treasure Beach way and buy fish, and melon and tomatis and skellion, all those things what them Saint Bess people did grow, what nobody else was growing those time. And Arnold is one of the people he used to deal with.

When Arnold start put question, me never interested, because Arnold was a hard-back man and me was just a little bit of a girl. Used to ride with my Daddy sometimes for I was the youngest and he love me dearly. And I used to like travelling perch up on my Daddy dray, that time I boasy can't done, but I never like that part of the world he used to go to and me never like those St. Elizabeth red people. But after a while me just get used to Arnold, he know how to make me laugh, and my Daddy think highly of him. "That is a young fellow with nuff intelligence," my Daddy used to say. "Plenty ambition, girl. You can't do better." So my Daddy was happy when I marry Arnold.

When we married first, I did go to live at Arnold house, but me not lying, me could never get used to those people, no matter them was fambly now. Never could like them at all. And them never like me, that's a fact, for they just don't like black people.

So I pull Arnold and I pull him and I never stop till he agree to leave that place and come with me to my Daddy land in the hills. So he come and I will say he make the best of it. He never say anything, but every chance him get he would go down to Treasure Beach and he would come back with fish and smelling of the sea. He never once blame me for nothing though, wasn't that kind of man, not even when I never have no children. I used to tell him I don't need more pickney than him the way he go on foolish sometimes. I tell you, that man can make me bus some big laugh. When I bother him, he say, "A gone leave you, a swimming to Treasure Beach," and then he carry on as if he swimming. Moving his hands and feet any which way. He mek me laugh till water come a mi eye. What a foolish man though ee.

Arnold go on too bad sometime. Now you can tell me why he lying there in the sun-hot in the middle of the Ba'ma grass?

You see him water boots? One of them fall off already and the other soon come off. Is stubborn he stubborn why they fall off, you know. Because he always buying things larger than him size. Though him is such a little man, I think in him head he see himself as big as a king. If I didn't buy his clothes for him, nothing would ever fit him right. He swear even his foot bigger than it is and when he did go to buy a new pair of boots Saturday, I warn him to get the right size for I know how he stay. And lo and behold, he come back with a pair of water boots there that you could see was too big. He so stubborn, he argue with me say, no, water boots supposed to be big. Put them on this morning to leave for his ground and see here now, it look like these big boots mek him stumble and fall, why else he lying there on the ground? Him hat and all fall off. Lying there making me think is joke he joking.

Is what Miss Dorcas big son did call out to me just now when I was hanging out the clothes and he frighten me, he there bawling so loud? Why I can't remember? Lawd, my memory was always bad, from I was a young girl I forgetful. Is something Arnold tease me about all the time.

The boy say something about Arnold and I remember now I drop the clothes and run. My Father! I drop the good white clothes straight into the dutty ground. Is what happening to me poor soul, eh? And now I have more washing to do for Arnold new shirt soaking in blood and he lying here not saying a word and Shannon standing there like a snake and the people back off and standing over there fraid of Shannon and it can't be true what the boy run come tell me. It can't be true say Shannon shoot Arnold dead?

Arnold always say he want to die by the sea and is I take him away from where he wanted was to be. Jesus only know I have to take him back there. He can't just die here so.

Arnold, come mi love. Let me help you sit up. Look. Look over there and see a great wave rising. It coming from the sea. It bringing the whole of Treasure Beach rising up to meet you. See the boat them there. And your fisherman friend them. Festus and Marse George and Tata Barclay and Lloydie. See yu mother Miss Adina and see Grandy Maud, your sister Merteen, little Shelly your niece and baby Jonathan. Just sit up and look nuh, and stop play dead. You too jokify man, and everybody watching. Open yu eye and look, Arnold, if you think a lie. See the great wave there. Coming over the mountain. Coming to carry us home.

The Lizardy Man and His Lady

B ANG! BANG! You dead!"

"No. I shoot you first!"

"No. I first say you dead."

"Well, I'm not playing with you again. You're not playing fair."

"Is you cheating."

"No. Is you."

～～

Jesus Mary and Joseph! What wrong with you children ee? Shelly-Ann, what kind of noise that you making in the people house? Roger, why you have to go on like big man so? You know what, the two of you better sit down quiet and watch TV. Eh, Miss Ersie? We don't want to hear another peep out of you. If I have any more bother from you, Miss Shelly-Ann, home you go. And I not bringing you back to play with Roger again if is so you going to behave. When I come here to visit Miss Ersie, we don't want no noise and confusion in we head.

———

. . . as I was saying, Miss Ersie, and this is the Lord own truth, if it wasn't for the little one there, me would leave long time, you know. Go right back to mi owna yard. For certain things people like me and you shouldn't have no call to put up with at our age. Seh what? Yes mi'dear. Getting worse every day. You lucky you have a nice family like this to work for. That's what I was used to one time too. But sometimes you can't predict how things will turn out ee? Like when you see what can happen to some people good-good pickney. When you see how them can turn down. A walla-walla with so-so bad company. Me seh, her mother would have belly-come-down pain if she could see the class of people fe har pickney a mix with these last days.

Seh what? You hear him was in prison in Miami one time? Fe ganja? A same so me did hear. A whole planeload. And now them say him in the other business there big-big. What them call it? Eh-hm. The coke and the crack and all them sinting. Imagine eh, mam? Is that me big-woman have to live with. But you see me here, although me have to live in the same house, you have to say is fe him money paying me, still and all, Miss Ersie, me walk far from him, you know. Me do me job and me say, "Yes, sir," "No, sir," to everything and me swallow mi tongue. Not that him really exchange more than two word with anybody. Him not a talking man. And them seh you can eat with the devil if you carry a long spoon. So my spoon well long.

Seh what? Her family? Lawd, mi'dear, them don't business with her again. At all 'tall. Then you never know seh the family cut her off? Me never tell you? Well, what I should say is, she refuse to have one single thing to do with them from the time she leave the husband and go move in with the first fellow there. Didn't like what her mother have to say one bit. So she just cut herself off. Well, that one didn't last very long, I can tell you. And is a good thing her family don't even know the half of it. Suppose them did know the kind of life she was a lead?

Well, me stick with her through thick and thin, move up and down town with her, for who else she have to look after little Shelly-Ann? And me not lying, some time there she don't even have money to pay mi wages. I don't even know what we eat. From she leave the husband, she suck salt, I tell you. Suck salt. From one man to the next till she meet up with this one and them move into the house here. Well, him seem to have plenty money to throw around. Give her more gold chain and ring and all them sinting. Satellite dish pon the roof. Plenty food pon table. She jump inna plane gawn a Miami every two minute. But for all that, there is other kind of crosses, as me and you know, mi'dear.

Well, yes, she did get a job when she leave the husband. Job here, job there, but she never stay long in any of them. For Miss Ella nuh too use to work, and me nuh think they was paying her too much money for all that. And the kind of place we had was to move to! Imagine a woman of that pedigree living in one little flat in the back of people yard. It wasn't what she was used to, I can tell you. But is she make her bed, so she had was to lie on it. Plenty time, when she feeling down down down, when she just a cry can't done, them time me say: "Miss Ella, go and make your peace with your parents. Go to your mother and father and beg their forgiveness. They will take you back in for they love you regardless. They will look after you and Shelly-Ann. You can't continue to live so."

Miss Ersie, I tell you those time my heart really go out to her. She sucking salt. But she say no, was too proud to humble herself.

Me tell you. You see her there now a mix up herself with every kind of riff-raff? You wouldn't believe what a pretty pickney she used to be. The class of family that girl come from. Born into mi hand, you have to say. Is me raise and grow her. And when she get married, is me her mother beg go with her to go set up her owna house.

Her mother say to me, "Gatha, I don't know how I myself going to manage without you. But Ella need you more than me now. Is no use sending one of these foolish little young girls that don't know one thing to work for her. Is you going have to show her everything about keeping house." Well, I never want to leave my old mistress, for is twenty-five years I work with her, leave my mother yard as a young little pickney to go there. And me and her have our ups and downs, for she have her ways there like all of them. But I not lying to you, she still better than most, for she treat me fair and square. Couldn't say she never fair. So since she ask me, I go with Miss Ella. For is big man she marry, you know. Expecting her to entertain all twenty people to dinner party one night and them sort of thing.

Well she did know how to look pretty and dress up herself, but that is all she know. I really have to say I don't know what she woulda do without me. And that is not boasify. Is the Lord own truth. For me not lying, Miss Ella get married but she couldn't do one single thing, spoil like all them other rich people pickney. Have somebody walk and pick up after them from morning till night. Left to me, she wouldn't grow so. She woulda learn to do something for herself. But as far as her mother and father concern, like how them don't have no other children, the sun rise and set on her. "Gatha, don't worry. Ella will learn in time," is what fe har mother used to say every time I quarrel about how Miss Ella keep her room, how she just throw down everything on the floor for me to pick up. I never like it at all and I did raise my voice to her sometime, for I didn't feel it was right to bring up a girl pickney so. Eh, Miss Ersie? Don't you feel seh girl pickney must learn to look after themself, rich or no rich? Nuh so! But is them spoil her. The parents spoil her from she born. That is the Lord own truth.

❧

"Let's play house."
"Okay. This is my briefcase. Where are my car keys?"
"What you want briefcase for?"
"Because I'm the daddy and the daddy always has a briefcase."
"My daddy don't."
"Not true. I see him with briefcase."
"Who?"

"Your daddy. I see him at your house already get into his car with a briefcase."

"You mean Mr. Lizardy Man. That man is not my daddy!"

"Why you call him so?"

"Promise you won't tell?"

"Promise."

"Because he look just like a lizard, ha ha."

"Shelly-Ann, you too foolish. Lizard green. He not green."

"He wear lizard-skin shoes."

"They don't have lizard-skin shoes. How much lizard you think they would have to kill to make one pair of shoes?"

"Well, I don't business with that. That's what he wear. And he just lie there all day long watching TV with his lizard-skin shoes sticking out over the edge of the couch. The living room dark like anything for he pull the curtain. And he just lie there all day long. Without moving. Don't move at all. Look just like an ugly croaking lizard."

"So what your mother would be doing with a lizard-man, then?"

"She's not my mother."

"Shelly-Ann! You story. Is your mother. I hear my mother say so, and she don't lie. Gatha say she is your mother. I even hear you call her Mummy plenty time. So how come all of a sudden she's not your mother?"

"She not my mother."

"So who is she then?"

"She is the Lizardy Man's lady, ha ha."

"Cho. You too foolish. We playing this game or what? Or you're just going to stand there the whole day telling lie?"

"Don't say that. I don't tell lie."

"You do too. You just told some fantastic ones."

"Didn't."

"Did."

"Didn't."

"Did."

"Didn't."

— —

Jesus Mary and Joseph! Children! Shelly-Ann, you shouting again. You know what, Miss, one more peep out of you and I lick you till you fennay today. You hear me? Miss Ersie, I really can't take these rude children, you know. Next time I come back for a chat, I am coming by my own self. And that will serve you right, Shelly-Ann.

— —

. . . anyway, Miss Ersie, me feel seh, plenty something a go on. Me can't say me see anything, you know, but nobody can convince me that she not taking some of them something herself. Me never see her tek nothing, me can't lie and say me see it, though me know them smoke the weed there hard-hard. But that is nothing. She been doing that long time now, long before she meet this man here. But me know seh, these last few months, she really change. Sometimes you see her there, she just out of this world. Just like the other one there. The man. Is two weeks now him nuh leave the house, you know. The two of them. Lock up inside the house there day and night. Me not lying to you. Me feel something gwine happen. Is like the two of them just waiting for something to happen. And she not paying the little pickney one mind. Almost have to say the child don't have mother again. It break my heart to see how she treating little Shelly-Ann. That's why she get rude and giving so much trouble. The little child can't even go near the mother now, she push her away, tell her to go and play. Have no time for her at all. Sometime is as if she don't even see her.

Me not lying, me would really like to get out. For from my mother born and grow me, I never mix up in nothing yet. And me would gone long time, Miss Ella or no Miss Ella. But me can't bring myself to leave the little one here. For if it wasn't for me, she wouldn't have a soul to mind her.

I am a woman that know how to keep my own counsel. But I decide I going to take it upon my head to write to her grand-mother. Going to send her a letter. Eh, what you think, Miss Ersie? Don't you think I have every right to put the case before her? Write her and beg her no matter what, she is please to come for the child?

Well, there you have it. You right, the child have a father even though she don't see him from one year to the next. But is still her father. Maybe he is the right one to come. I am going to write Miss Ella mother and put the case and she will know what to do. For you have to say now Shelly-Ann don't have no mother. Mother don't business with her at all 'tall. Mother head gone, you have to say, the way she a behave. And me can't carry on no more. Me nuh care if Miss Ella vex when she find out. Me can't deal with her and her jingbang life no longer. For she not the same person me did agree to go to work for. Is like a different somebody. This situation just can't go on.

~ ~

"Shelly-Ann, you know what?"

"What?"

"Your father there. All right, then. The Lizardy Man. You know he is a dealer?"

"A what?"

"A dealer. I don't know is what exactly. But is a bad thing. I hear my mother and father talking about it. They don't like how he living on the same street with us. Say plenty bad things going to happen."

"I know one bad thing already."

"What?"

"It's a secret."

"But I just tell you a secret."

"Okay then. The Lizardy Man have some guns."

"Guns? You mean he have more than one?"

"Eh-hm."

"What kind of guns?"

"I don't know."

"How they stay?"

"Well, one is little, like what the detectives use on TV. The bad guys, too. When they say 'Hands up' or something like that. The one they put to your head and go click-click. The Lizardy Man have one of those. He have it with him all the time."

"Cho, Shelly-Ann, that is nothing. My daddy has one of those. He sleeps with it in the bedroom. In case he has to shoot a thief."

"No thief coming to our house. You know is four bad dogs we have. Doberman at that."

"Shelly-Ann, you know we have bad dogs, too. Ridgeback worse than Doberman any day. Badder than bad. But thief can still come. That's why my daddy has his gun."

"Well, we have security fencing. And electric gate. You don't have that. Anybody can just drive into your yard. Our gate only open when the Lizardy Man drive up and press something in the car and it make the gate open. Or else you have to press a buzzer and the Lizardy Man will talk to you from the house. Then he decide if he is going to let you in or not. Nobody can just drive in as they like."

"So how the other gun stay, Shelly-Ann?"

"He have another one hide in the clothes closet in the bedroom. Is like what the police carry."

"What? A M-16?"

"I don't know is what. Same like you see the police driving around in their jeep with."

"M-16, Shelly-Ann. To raatid!"

— ◆ —

Well, Miss Ersie, I must go. Time to get dinner ready. Not that anybody in that house bother to eat. Food just cook and it throw out. The dogs eat better than the people. Pure raw meat him feed them on, you know. Every day the one Troja there, the bwoy that work for him, every day Troja gone a butcher for the living raw meat to feed the dog them. Well, me glad that that is not part of my job, having anything to do with them animal. For me naw lie, Miss Ersie, well, you come up there and you see for yourself, you see how them stay. Don't them is like savage, mam, like real wild animal? Me can't even stand to look at them for me know seh a nuh so dog suppose to look.

Anyway, is really gone a gone this time. Where is this child now? Shelly-Ann, say goodbye to Roger, dear, and come. Yes, we have to go now. No, Shelly-Ann, you can't stay here with Roger, you have you owna house to go to. Listen nuh, pickney, don't form fool with me, you hear. What you crying for? You want a give you something to make you cry? Hush. I will bring you back tomorrow to play with Roger. I promise. Say goodbye to Miss Ersie now. That's a good girl. Well, a gone, mi'dear. And I going to do what a tell you. Tomorrow, you hear.

❦

Lawd, Shelly-Ann, what you bawling for? Your mother will think a beating you, man. Come, mek me dry yu eye, you can't go home to your mother looking like this. Seh what, seh you don't have no mother? How you can say such a thing, chile, and you have yu good-good mother at yu yard. Oh, my poor little innocent lamb, you must never say such a thing, dear. I know she not paying you too much mind these days but, Shelly-Ann, you is a big girl now so you must understand. Your mother not well, so you must try and see with her. She will soon get better and treat you nice and loving the way she always treat you. Say

what wrong with her? She just not well, Shelly-Ann. She have
big people complaint. Say what that is? Listen nuh, pickney,
what is wrong with you? Why you have to ask question so? Just
don't bother to try my spirit, you hear?

Lawd have mercy! Shelly-Ann, stop! Stop. Stop. Stop. Right
there. Don't go one step further. Shelly-Ann, you hear me?
Come back. Aright. Don't move from here, chile. Stand right
here so. I don't like what I see. Shelly-Ann, how the gate throw
wide open so? You ever see the gentleman leave the gate open
yet? And him car right there in the garage. And where the dog
them, Shelly-Ann? Is who open the gate? You think the dog
them run weh? Jesus save us, is what this on me today? Girl,
something just tell me we not to go in there. We not to go in
there at all. Come. We going right back down to Miss Ersie.
We can phone your mother from there. Something just tell me
we not to go in. Don't like what a seeing. Shelly-Ann, what
you think happen to the dog them, and the gate wide open?
Jesus, what a autoclaps if them loose on the street and we buck
them up! Come, pickney. Mek we tek foot and run, you hear?

"What happen, Shelly-Ann, why you come back?"

"I don't know, Roger. Gatha say I must come and play with
you."

"O.K. What do you want to play?"

"I don't know. Anything."

"What about 'Police and Criminal'? Stay right here. I'm going to get my gun. M-16 badder than Criminal. You can only have your knife, so Police going to shoot you dead, Mister Badman! Eh, where is your knife, Shelly-Ann? You playing this game or what? You better go and borrow one from the kitchen. But don't make Ersie see you."

"Roger?"

"Yes."

"You know what? Something happening at our yard."

"What?"

"I don't know. We never go in. Gatha gone to get Ersie to phone my mother."

"How you mean?"

"Gatha say we not to go in. For the gate was wide open. And the Lizardy Man car was there."

"So what if the gate open?"

"I tell you already, that gate never open. Only if the Lizardy Man press a button and open it himself. Even for us, Mummy and me and Gatha, when we want to come and go. He or Troja always there to open the gate. But they never ever leave it open. As soon as you gone through, they close it again."

"So what you think happen, Shelly-Ann?"

"I don't know."

"My daddy said something bad was going to happen."

"Gatha said so, too."

"Maybe they gone out and forget to lock back the gate."

"No. Roger?"

"What?"

"I know one thing that happen. Something bad."

"Bad like what?"

"Well, I don't know if Gatha did see. Gatha so frighten. But I see. Roger, I see two dead dog lying on the lawn."

"What! Doberman can't dead! You crazy?"

"Maybe bad man come. Kill off the Lizardy Man. And the Lady."

"You mean your mother? Stop joking, Shelly-Ann."

"The lady is not my mother. I tell you that already."

"Shelly-Ann, you gone crazy? What you hit me for?"

"Is not my mother. Is not my mother. Is not my mother. Don't I tell you that?"

"Stop it, Shelly-Ann. You're going to wreck the place."

"You just wait and see, Mister Roger Know-It-All. My mother's going to drive up any minute now. My mother's taking me to Miami to shop. Buy me all kinds of toys. Better than yours. Better than everybody's in the whole wide world. Then I don't have to come over here and play with your old bruck."

"Shelly-Ann, what you doing? Stop flinging my things about. Give me that. Oh Lord, not my mother's lamp. Oh no, Shelly-Ann! Please! Gatha! Ersie! Come quick!"

— ⌒ —

Jesus Mary and Joseph! Oh my poor little Shelly-Ann.

The Glass-Bottom Boat

She was sitting in her slip at the dressing table, getting ready to go out. Where, he knew, she would not even bother to say. Or, if he asked, as he might have done at some earlier point in time, she would answer in her crisp, new voice: "I am going to Joy's." Or, "I am going to class," "I am going to town," in a tone that was really saying, "Mind your own business."

He sat in his chair in the little living room from which he could look directly at her in the bedroom and, watching her, he wondered at all her busyness nowadays with pots and jars and lotions when so little result was obtained. What upset him the most was that her hair-combing ritual had come to an end, and what was she without her hair? That was one of the things he had loved about her: she had a thick head of hair, natural, unstraightened, which she used to comb out slowly every night, rub with oil, and then twist into small bumps all over her head. That gave her such a sweet fresh-faced innocence as she came to bed, he imagined every night she was born anew. Then in the mornings before going to work she would take out the tiny bumps and, with innumerable hairpins, work the hair into an elaborate pinned-up style which, he knew, was very unfashionable, but was one of the endearing things about her, making her what she was, though he had never told her so. Imagine his shock, then, when she came home one day with her beautiful natural hair cut off. Barbered. Chopped into the short mannish style they were calling the Afro or whatever. He was so stunned, he thought a stranger had walked through the door, and that night he had to take a whole tablespoon of bicarbonate of soda to settle his stomach. Sick like a dog all night. Headache all day. Chopped off her hair like that. He was outraged that she hadn't even bothered to say anything to him beforehand, as if, like so many things she did nowadays, she was doing it deliberately to show her contempt for him.

But although her action raised such intense feelings in him, he said nothing at all, merely looked interested when she came in with her new hair, for he was not accustomed to argue or even to express strong opinions. And when he did voice an opinion, no one was ever much interested in what he had to say. Except for her. But that was once upon a time.

Well, he couldn't help thinking, how things have changed, eh? And when he reflected on that, the dark feeling, that sensation of falling, falling endlessly, came over him again, and he had to sit and hold his head down until he got back enough strength to go and lie on the bed.

He was still lying there when she had finished dressing.

She muttered something – he didn't catch what it was – and the small frame house shook as she went out and slammed the door.

He didn't know how long she had been working in the typing pool before he saw her. One day Miss Lindsay was sick and this Miss Pearson was sent to help out. He was surprised to see someone like her there. Manston Dunn was one of the biggest companies in the country. Starting out as importers of rice and codfish, they had grown to become a conglomerate with investments in just about everything. And though their head office was the same dark and gloomy warren on the waterfront where the founders had started out sixty years before, it was still regarded as a highly desirable place to work. The secretaries tended to be attractive and smartly dressed, graduates of the best schools or, at the very least, they were of the best class.

Sybil Pearson looked extremely young, with wide-set eyes and high cheekbones, and had a pretty enough face, if you really bothered to look and if she had bothered to smarten herself up. But from the way she dressed and carried herself she was hardly the type of girl you would expect to find in an office of that kind. She spoke well enough, but in an exaggerated, stilted kind of way, as if proper English was still new to her and required intense effort, and she made the odd mistake in grammar and pronunciation, which the other girls found hilarious.

Her appearance proclaimed her station more than anything

else. Her thick hair was piled in rolls on her head in an unstylish way; she wore no makeup. He liked to look at the women in the office, the way they dressed, would tease them in an avuncular way about their high heels and short skirts. But this girl! However did she come to be hired? Her clothing was definitely of the type who proclaimed themselves "Christian," those self-righteous women who had nothing better to do than to go to church and prayer meetings every night and act holier than other people. They had never had any of that type of person on the office staff before, and he wondered what the world – or the personnel office – was coming to.

She wore unfashionably long skirts of dark, heavy materials, and white or pastel-coloured blouses with high necks and long sleeves. She wore thick stockings and big clumsy shoes. Her only adornment was the occasional hairclip or an unattractive brooch which she often wore pinned at her neck. Her manner matched her dress: she was awkward and soft-spoken and diffident. He was amused to see that she walked with her knees locked close together as if she had to protect some treasure there, as if, he thought, the clothes weren't doing that well enough. She was tall and big-boned but slim and coltish, as if she hadn't yet become a woman, filled out as she should.

He was surprised to find that she was quick and efficient. You showed her something just once, and she caught on right away. Best of all, she was quiet as a mouse; you were hardly even aware of her presence. How unlike Miss Lindsay, who was a constant source of irritation. He attributed his bad stomach directly to having Miss Lindsay near him, day in, day out, every working day of his life. Miss Lindsay and he had been together in the firm for over thirty years, and though he was not a man of strong passion, every moment of that time he wished he had never set eyes on her. She had grown older and sloppier and more unattractive with each passing year, and remained the most incapable, inconsiderate, inefficient, annoying woman he had ever known.

Nobody else wanted Miss Lindsay and he had ended up getting stuck with her, because, unlike the others, he was too weak to protest. He was also a little afraid of her. Of her sharp tongue. And her tears. Her tears were what kept her at Manston Dunn, would probably keep her there until retirement. Old Man Dunn was also sentimental about her because her father had been one of those who had been there at the start, who had invested his own money and laboured with Manston and Dunn to get the new firm going. Just as his own father had done. He forced aside the thought that Old Man Dunn kept him on for the same reasons Miss Lindsay was kept on, despite her bungling incompetence, her fierce temper, and her eccentricities – sentiment and loyalty.

Well, nobody could say he was incompetent: he was in charge of all the stationery, office supplies, and machines, hiring and firing the cleaners and office boys and supervising their work, seeing about the company cars. Nobody could say he was not on top of everything in his portfolio; he kept everyone on their toes counting paper clips and pencils, scrutinizing with great detail the garage and gas-station bills, the machine repair charges.

But although he could not express it to anyone, he some-times felt wanting, as though he were living only half a life, in his job, at home; the other half he was barely aware of, but felt it hovering beneath the surface like some astonishing sea crea-ture, waiting for him to claim it.

He had started out as a clerk at Manston Dunn – both his father and Old Man Dunn expected that he would; they wanted their children to enter the firm and eventually take over, so he was only one of several of the second generation with the names of the original directors. Sometimes it did occur to him that, in the thirty-odd years, what he actually did for the company hadn't changed much – though his title and pay packet changed, Old Man Dunn saw to that. But the other sons, in time, had left to go on to better things or been pro-moted far more rapidly than he, were sharing now in the power and decision-making, were moving into bigger offices or outside to head up one or other of the new companies Manston Dunn was always acquiring. Even the grandsons were moving up now.

He never had the nerve to question any of this – why he was not chosen to head up this or that – thinking that if he were patient and worked hard, his time would come. Of late though, he got the feeling that he had from the start been working his way into a dead end. What had happened? How had he got that way? He wasn't sure. Sometimes he reflected that maybe it was the burden of being the second generation of the new middle class. His father, all their fathers, had started with nothing, pulled themselves up by their bootstraps (as his father had been fond of telling him). By the time he came along, what was there to struggle for? He had been born into a nice house on a nice street with friends who were like him, went to a fine school, knew that, unlike most of his schoolmates, he already had a job, a future mapped out. But then, he thought, all the other Manston Dunn heirs came from the same sort of background, so why was he the only one not moving? Was it because of his father? He never liked to think of his father if he could help it. As a small boy he worshipped him. His awareness that in spite of being the eldest child and the only son he had come to be the source of bitter disappointment to his father only dawned gradually.

Eric Johns, Sr., having spent the money to send his son to what he regarded as the best school in the land, the school he himself would have wanted to attend if his family's finances had permitted, set out to live his own unfulfilled ambitions through his son. Jamaica College boys were brains, they said, so he'd fantasize that Eric, Jr., would get top grades all through school and go on to win the Island Scholarship. When Eric consistently came in passing, but always just, he projected his dreams for the boy into athletics. He could see himself inviting all his friends to go to the championships to watch his son, the class-one athlete; to see him play football on a Manning Cup team, see him captain the First Eleven. When Eric showed no aptitude for track, football, or cricket, his father lowered his sights somewhat – he taught him to swim and saw him as the island champion; he sent him to the rifle range to learn marksmanship – and saw him representing his country at Bisley.

Eric, it turned out, was good at nothing except singing and music – talents he got from his mother. In fact, he was like his mother, soft, not very demanding. Unlike his father, who, for all his affability, shouted and tyrannized to get his way (either at home or office), who had an unspeakably cruel tongue which he used like a whip at times (on his employees, on his wife or his son), who drove everyone as hard as he drove himself.

Eric was happy when his three younger sisters got old enough to make their father totally lose interest in him. The girls were far more gratifying in every way – they were bright and teasing and combative and constantly challenged their father, kept him on his toes, kept him young, gave him something to boast about; they provided for him the type of family he wanted. Whereas, before, Eric had been the sole target of a cruel inquisition whenever his father was home, the object of slighting remarks and offhand lectures, now he was not even expected to venture a remark. If at the dinner table he spoke at all, his father would ignore him, sometimes rudely interrupt him.

Eric didn't really mind his father's indifference; he was relieved that he was no longer the focus of his attentions, and thereafter tried to be the focus of nobody's. If he spoke at all, he got into the habit of offering only the mildest, most inoffensive remark, tried to make himself pleasant by developing a repertoire of harmless old-world flatteries for women, a hearty cheerfulness for men, and never got argumentative or raised his voice.

He was happy enough to go off to his job and, after he got married, to return in the evenings to the peace and quiet of his own home. His wife, Elise, was the lively one in their family and he was entirely happy to leave the running of the house and the raising of their three boys to her.

Occasionally she would remind him of some cocktail party or dinner they were invited to, and he'd dutifully go, and have a few drinks and smile and compliment the ladies and make a few remarks that were so trite and inane, people paid attention only because Eric was such a kind, good-hearted man, so attractive and courteous in a nice old-fashioned way, and no one wanted to hurt his feelings.

Most days, he'd go home and watch television and go to bed, and then wake up the next morning and read the newspaper and go to work. On weekends, he pottered around the house, for he liked to tinker with appliances, mend things that were broken, fix dripping taps. Every Sunday morning he went to service at Parish Church, where he had been christened, married, and expected to be buried. He had been going to morning service since he was old enough to remember, and he continued to go, mainly because he liked the sound of organ music.

⁓ ⁓

Miss Lindsay, who had seemed to be taking more and more sick leave, after one long absence never came back to the office. Miss Pearson came in and took over her desk, placed on it a jam jar with a climbing plant which had stayed stunted and yellow in the typing pool, but which here, by the window, began a new life of slow but rampant growth.

Nobody thought anything of Miss Pearson taking over from Miss Lindsay. Going to work for Eric Johns wasn't regarded as something desirable – he was generally seen as a harmless bore who sat and shuffled papers all day long and dealt with the office boys and cleaning women and drivers. Everyone could see that, despite his name and the fact that his father had been one of the directors, he wasn't going anywhere, which meant that neither would any secretary of his.

Miss Pearson herself was regarded by the other secretaries as a bore, so good it irritated you, they said to each other, so annoying with her constant smiles and words of cheer and her awful clothes. And that hairdo! Without saying so, everyone was relieved when she no longer sat in the main office where all the visitors could see her; most of the other girls had found it a bit embarrassing, as if the maid had wandered in by mistake and taken a seat at a typing desk. She and Johns deserve each other, some wit remarked, and everyone snickered in agreement.

He got used to having Miss Pearson around the office, began to admire her calm efficiency, even the way she dressed and wore her hair, which seemed to declare that she was, simply, who she was. Occasionally, he gave her a lift home. Because she lived downtown near the office he got into the habit of taking her home whenever they worked late, or, if it was raining, treating her the way he would treat any other woman, getting out to open the car door, waiting until she was safely inside before driving off. He never thought anything of this (he did it because he was fundamentally a courteous man) any more than he thought about the way he defended Miss Pearson at office gatherings when, it seemed, everyone conspired to tease her, to seduce her from the straight and narrow path on which she was so obviously placed. The salesmen at Christmas parties were particularly obnoxious:

"Cho, Miss P, man. Just one little sip of wine?" one of them would coax her. She would smile at the circle of men around her and hang down her head.

"But, Miss P, don't they say in the Bible that Jesus did turn water into wine?" another would say. "Then if wine was a bad thing, you think he would do that?"

Miss Pearson would continue to lower her head and smile her bashful smile and he would march into the circle and rescue her.

His father had been, like Old Man Dunn and most of the other men from the early days of the company, a self-made man. That's how businessmen started out in those days – serving behind the counter, or visiting their customers themselves, going down to the wharves to clear their own goods, taking risks and playing games. He remembered that when he was a very small child his father had got around the city on a bicycle – and there was no shame attached. Was his generation the first one to feel shame if they did not have those things which nowadays seemed necessary to impress other people – the car, the house, the clothes, the old school tie, the posh accent? As the company grew, these men, including his own father, had prospered, had become prominent in social and civic life: the leaders.

And he? Hadn't he prospered, too? He lived in the right area, he drove a good car, his wife worked and she also drove a late-model car which she had paid for herself. Elise was an office administrator and was good at her job, an attractive, efficient woman who served on committees, who liked to go to cocktail parties and dinners and make the social round. She came from the same sort of background as he, and when they got married, everyone remarked that it was a good match. He was handsome and well-mannered and was expected to go far. She was thought to be the perfect wife for a rising young executive.

He occasionally felt guilty when he thought that perhaps he hadn't risen as far as she had expected, and that the good things – their house, their children's education, their entire life style – were due not so much to his own efforts as to the legacies his father and Elise's father had left them. It made him uncomfortable, as if these fathers were standing there on the other side still laughing at him, still heckling him for being a lesser man than they were.

- ~

How had it all begun? he asked himself, and he really couldn't say. Everything had simply happened, as if he and Sybil Pearson had found themselves on the same trajectory, on a path which, once taken, had to be followed down to wherever it led, even if it meant falling and falling. Now why had he thought that? Hadn't it been good there for a while? Hadn't it made him feel young again and bursting with possibilities, hadn't he felt somewhere along the way that his other self, the part of him which had been lurking outside his life, had finally been dragged into the light?

Now he realized that the feeling of falling, of having no real centre, had begun long before he had ever met Sybil Pearson. But it was around the time she first came into his life that he had begun to feel frail, like a plant that hadn't been properly rooted. Going home at night to an empty house with his dinner in the oven, he began to get the feeling that his life, his very existence, was so insubstantial that it hardly mattered to anyone. Perhaps it had to his mother, but she had died a long time ago.

His wife spoke to him less and less, her painted face seemed to grow harder with the years, her eyes cold and dismissive; his sons had suddenly become men (two were at university and one was doing accounting), had changed so rapidly that it was difficult for him to keep track of who was who. He continued to go to the parties, his wife continued to have people over, but he moved among them like a ghost. Even his church-going was beginning to feel thin and meaningless, as if the organ music had suddenly lost its sonorous booming sound and instead resembled the tinkling of a harpsichord.

He sometimes felt that he was looking at everything as through the "glass-bottom boats" he used to ride in as a child when his father took them to Montego Bay. Ordinary in all other ways, these boats had a square of thick glass let into the bottom through which he could see, in a wavering and fractured light, another, stranger, more magical life below. For months after returning home from one of these excursions he would imagine himself sitting in the boat, feeling lulled by its gentle bobbing on the turquoise water of the bay, and looking down to see the violently luminescent fish darting in and out of a flourishing garden of coral, sea fans, and waving vegetation.

Sometimes, now, he had this desire to test himself, to see whether he really existed for anyone, and he would change his routine for a while. Although he was not a drinking man, after work he would drop in at the cricket club where he had been a member since the age of twenty-one, though he hardly ever went there. He would sit at the bar with the set of senior civil servants who drank there every day, men he had gone to school with, but he noticed that once they greeted him they went back to drinking and talking shop and never saw him again, not even when he left. Going home, he'd find nobody there to remark on his lateness.

Increasingly, he found himself getting into his car after work, intending to go home, but without being conscious of doing so he would go to the hills and park at the lookout and stare at the city below without seeing anything, for how long he could never say. Or the tang of the sea would come to him and he would find himself out at Port Royal, sitting by himself in a restaurant by the water, eating fish, or parked on the side of the Palisadoes away from the harbour, watching the breakers.

At the office, his mind drifted. Sometimes he would stare at gas coupons or machine bills for hours and wonder what he was doing there, what would happen if one day he dematerialized through the grimy window which opened onto the lane, floated like vapour across the harbour, and became one with the salty air over the open sea. Would anyone at Manston Dunn even note his passing?

More and more he began to think that Miss Pearson was the only one who had any awareness of his presence, who took note of whether or not he was even there at all, as a living breathing human being, who would remark if he evaporated from the scene as his old secretary Miss Lindsay had done some time ago.

Miss Pearson had hardly changed over the years, no mark of passing time showed. She had the same soft eyes and mild expression, though she wore glasses now. While she was still modest and shy, and he didn't talk much, they would sometimes exchange remarks. But most of the time in the office they achieved a companionable silence; Miss Pearson appeared as comfortable with her lot as he seemed with his. At Christmas and other occasions he took her out to lunch — something all the bosses did for their secretaries from time to time. He appreciated more and more the way she greeted him in the mornings with a bright smile and a "How are you, Mr. Johns?" He came to look forward to the words. Every evening before leaving she asked him if there was anything else he needed.

When his mind wandered, the sight of her would bring him

back to reality. More and more he found her appealing, admired the old-fashioned upswept hairdo, the habit she had of holding her head a little to one side when anyone spoke to her, her smile guileless as a child's, her consistency of dress and manner, which gave her a sense of being rooted, of certainty.

He wasn't aware that there was anything carnal in his feelings for her (that was the word he used to himself) and was probably as surprised as she was the night he gave her a lift from the office and instead of taking the turnoff to her house continued on the highway until they got to the Palisadoes, where he drove onto the beach, stopped the car, and took her in his arms. It didn't occur to him then that she'd said nothing, expressed no surprise whatsoever at anything he did, not even when he started to remove the brooch from her neck, unbutton her blouse.

She said nothing as he drove her home, except to ask him to drop her at the end of the street because she didn't want anyone to see him driving her home at that hour. And in the years that followed, that was the only thing she was concerned about. That nobody should see.

They were both so isolated from the mainstream of office life that they didn't even provoke gossip. No eyes were on them in the little corner room and nobody could imagine either of them having a romance, much less with each other. As soon as she found out she was pregnant she left the job and there was nobody there she kept up with. The gossip started only long after, when it got around that he had left his wife to live with her. Then it spread like wildfire.

Their affair might have gone on the way it had been going if she hadn't become pregnant. They hadn't been taking any precautions, so it was a wonder that something hadn't happened sooner. Even so, they were unprepared for it when it did happen, and it woke her out of her seemingly calm acceptance of things as they were and threw her into a state of panic and terror. All she could think of was the disgrace. What would Parson, her mother, the neighbours, her church sisters and brothers say? For despite their affair, she had never ceased her church-going, though as far as her church was concerned, she was now fallen, had engaged in deadly sin. Indeed, until she became pregnant, both had continued to live their normal lives in every way, except for those few hours after work snatched in his car.

So when one night as soon as they'd parked she had started to weep, it was so unexpected and unlike her that it threw him entirely, and it was some time before he got the story out of her. At first he felt shattered, not so much by the fact of her pregnancy, as by the enormity of what he had done: he had gone and ruined another person's life, a young woman who had been innocent and pure. But then, the idea of her pregnancy filled him with pleasure, for it came to him that this was an affirmation that he was as alive, as capable of action as everyone else. And it was in that elevated mood that he was able to comfort her with promises: "We'll get a house together. Have the baby. I'll ask my wife for a divorce. I'll marry you. We'll be happy together."

He had meant it, every word of it, had drawn her into his arms and held her tight; loving her wildly; he felt at last that he was recovering that lost side of himself. Felt that his life was becoming whole.

— ~

It wasn't his fault, surely, that nothing worked out the way he had planned. He had kept his promise and rented a house for them and moved in with her there to await the baby. He hadn't known that his wife would have been so angry, so vituperative, so vindictive even, when he told her he was moving out. He had thought that he occupied so little space in her life, she would hardly notice that he was no longer there. Perhaps she might not have noticed his going had he merely crept out one day and not come back, had he not been so clumsy about it, had he not told her – with greater enthusiasm than he had shown for anything before – about Miss Pearson and the baby.

She was outraged. As if to make him pay for, well, *demeaning* her in this way, she had managed to lay her hands on as much of their assets as possible. She instantly liquidated what she could, cleaned out their joint accounts, transferred everything to her name. He had planned to do what he considered the honourable thing, give her the house, some of their savings and investments. He calculated that he would still have enough to buy another, smaller house and live a reasonably comfortable life. But he found himself left with virtually nothing.

Which meant that he and Sybil could not continue to live in the house they first rented. He didn't tell her the whole truth, only that he was having some temporary financial problems which would soon be sorted out. It was she, in her practical manner, who found them another house, a modest bungalow in a neighbourhood he would never have dreamed of living in before, but it really didn't matter because that was the time when they were truly happy.

But there was no baby after all; she lost it in the sixth month.

━ ━

It struck him only later, when he had nothing to do but think, that once they began to live together they were like two castaways, for she had been severed from her old life as completely as he had been from his. Her entire world since childhood had been centred around her family and her church, and she lost both when they found out that she was pregnant and living with a married man. Her mother refused to have anything to do with her again, and she was publicly expelled from her church, which meant that the church sisters and brothers – her only friends – also forsook her. Yet, when he asked her once why she never went to church again, she only said, "They read me out."

"What do you mean?"

"Just that. They read me out. I can't go back. Well, unless I go to public confession and all that sort of thing."

He didn't know what "all that sort of thing" was and didn't want to ask, in case she thought he was prying. So she never talked about it. Nor did she say much when he asked her if she had told her mother about him and the baby and their living together.

"Yes, I wrote and told her."

He waited politely for her to say more, and when she didn't, was forced to ask, "So what did she say?"

"She says she doesn't want a daughter that is living a sweetheart life. Don't want a daughter living that kind of life."

He waited patiently for more, especially since the way she said the phrase gave it a ponderous sound. But they both sat there and nothing else was said, and soon she got up to prepare the dinner.

It wasn't until years later that he began to understand the magnitude of what had befallen her then; a severance that was probably even more traumatic than the death of the child. At the time, he had selfishly rejoiced that he no longer had to compete with her incessant church-going. That was the stage at which they were totally wrapped up in each other. And this lasted even after she lost the baby, for they agreed right away to have another.

Now, lying on the bed, he began to wonder: at what point had she decided that no baby was ever going to come? For that, surely, was the point at which she began to change. Was it the day she came home wearing lipstick? When she bought a jar of cold cream which she began to apply to her face every night? Was it the first dress she bought which showed her naked arms? The day she hemmed up her skirt and wore a belt which nipped in her waist?

All the changes had been introduced gradually, as if she

had had to work her way up to each one; there was nothing really startling about anything she did, and he liked what was happening to her. She was also putting on weight, filling out, becoming more of a woman, as if the baby had actually been born.

Though he never told her so, he was pleased that she never touched her hair, pleased every night as he sat on the bed and silently watched her as she combed out her thick long hair, parted and twisted it into the little bumps, put on her nightie and came to bed. That moment – with her sweet-faced inno-cence, her hair in those absurd little bumps, her scalp exposed at the parts which criss-crossed her head like a chequerboard – was when he felt for her the greatest tenderness, as if she were a rare flower and he the proud gardener entrusted with the deli-cate task of caring for her. He never felt inadequate to the task.

— —

But this was about the time the rumour mills had started, his wife having told the story to everyone around town, as if it were a joke, and his position in the office was never the same again. Junior Dunn, who had taken charge after Old Man Dunn retired, summoned him into his office one day. Al-though Junior didn't refer to Eric's private life, he was undeni-ably angry about something and bawled him out about his work – some silly mistake the auditors had brought to his attention. Humiliated, he crept out. He knew Dunn was angry because he had transgressed the code. It was all right for men of their class to have women on the side (everybody knew Junior had one stashed away in Northwinds Apartments), but they never had outside children, or at least never acknowledged them, and they conducted their business in such a way that they never, ever, humiliated their wives. Until then, he had never thought himself capable of humiliating anyone, much less Elise.

He was not surprised, then, when he was asked to take early retirement; they were reorganizing the office and it was that or redundancy. At least he would have a small pension.

He felt his life shrinking in every way. He and Sybil had to move to an even meaner frame house on a meaner street. At first he tried to keep up appearances, tried to maintain the car, so he could drive Sybil to and from work. But it got harder and harder and parts were expensive, so one day, regretfully, he had to let it go. For the first time in his life since he was a young schoolboy catching the tramcar, he was forced to use public transport, though he no longer went many places, after a time leaving home only if absolutely necessary. This wasn't based on any conscious decision; like so much of his life, this isolation simply crept up on him, growing day by day by slow accretions, until there was an imperceptible shift to a new position. He had stopped going to church soon after leaving his wife, as if that link with childhood no longer interested him; without Elise to push, he no longer took part in social activities and realized that, among their old friends, there was no one with whom he really wanted to keep up. The first phone calls and visits with his sisters and their families following the break with Elise had ended in tears, strident accusations, verbal abuse, so he simply dropped out of their lives. His only regret was his children. In giving up Elise, the house, his former existence, he had found no way of staying in touch, and as he had grown away from them they had grown up, assuming whole new lives. Thinking of his sons was the only time he felt sorrow, but, like everything else, he found it best to bury it deep inside him.

Once, shortly after he and Sybil had moved into the present house, a car had drawn up outside and a tall young man came out. At first he hadn't recognized his youngest son, Evan, and when he did, he rushed out with a cry. But once they'd exchanged greetings, they couldn't find the words to say anything to one another.

"You okay, Dad?" Evan finally said.

"Yes, fine, Son, everything's fine. You okay at home?"

"Sure, Dad."

After another, longer silence, Evan clumsily patted him on the back and got into the car. Then he leaned out and said, "Listen, Dad. If there's anything you want, if you need anything, anything at all, just call me, okay? Money or anything. I'm doing all right, you know." He couldn't even remember what Evan did.

He said, yes, yes, and Evan had driven off in his late-model car and he had bent down as if to tie his shoelace but really so that he could brush the tears away before entering the house.

"Who was that?" Sybil asked.

"Just my youngest son, Evan."

"Why you didn't bring him in?"

"He wasn't staying."

She left it at that, though he very much wanted her to ask

him about his son, his children, his unbearable loss, so he could talk about it. But she was not given to prying, any more than he was.

— ⁓

About a year after she lost the baby, and before the changes started, she told him she wanted to go to evening class to get her high-school qualifications in English. He realized that after knowing her for so many years he still knew nothing about her and the facts came out only after persistent questioning: she had come from the country and was one of five children whose father had died; her mother singlehandedly raised them on the earnings from a small piece of land. As the eldest child, she had had all their hopes pinned on her; it was expected that she would help the younger ones through school.

She had attended a junior secondary school in the nearby town and had graduated with her certificate in secretarial work. It was through her uncle, Mr. Dunn's gardener, that she had got the job at Manston Dunn. (He wondered if Junior Dunn had known of that connection.) He was amazed now that she had got in there with no academic qualifications at all, and yet had done so well.

He encouraged her to go back to night school, was proud to be able to help her with her lessons and in the process gently correct some of her speech faults. In a way, the studying of those years occupied them both, for he got as involved as she in her homework. Studying gave them a focus for their lives.

Still, there must have been something lacking, for on weekends when she finished cleaning and washing, he wondered
why she stirred so restlessly about the house, she who had
always been so quiet, so contained. They never went out or did
anything except watch television, but if she had wanted him to
take her out, she did not say. All she had to do was ask, and he
would have been so happy to do it.

More and more she spent time caring for her plants. She
never bothered with the yard, which had been neglected too
long to be reclaimed; she concentrated on her potted plants
which were now spilling beyond the stand he had built for
them on the verandah onto concrete blocks and even onto
the tiled floor itself. She was crazy about plants, often came
in from work with a slip wrapped in newspaper, would set it
in water or directly in the ground and it would take root and
sprout; if it gave trouble, she forced it to survive through her
ministrations. Her plants gave her contact with the neighbours: she would wander up the street and come back with
something growing in a condensed-milk tin; someone would
call at the gate and there would be an exchange; from time to
time conversations would take place over the fence about this
plant or that.

He was at first amused to discover that women found the
subject of plants as absorbing as that of children. But after a
while the whole thing began to irritate him, that she should
become so absorbed in her plants. Sometimes in the evenings
she would be out there until darkness fell, doing what, he never
could understand, moving from this one to that, clipping dead
leaves, watering, fertilizing, transplanting, ministering. Angry,

feeling abandoned, he would wonder: just how much attention did a silly plant need?

~ ~

He had begun to feel irritable about everything, although he never showed it. If she had bothered to look, she would have noticed some signs: a tightening around his jaw and a trembling of his hands. He hardly ate at all now and at nights tossed restlessly, feeling his life crumbling away. But she never noticed, in the same way he hadn't noticed for a long time the hardening of her features, a more positive lift to her body, a more powerful stride. She had put on so much weight the coltish body no longer existed; she was now heavy. She had totally abandoned the clothing of her youth, wore high heels and dresses which served to show off her body. Took to wearing bangles and chains and earrings. Only her old-fashioned hair remained to remind him of what she had been. He, rightly or wrongly, now attributed the changes to her attendance at university, where she was studying business management. She came and went at all hours and he could no longer keep track of her; she started to have friends, and car doors would slam and she would rush off, sometimes returning late at night after he had gone to bed.

For the first time since they had started living together, that feeling of displacement came back to him. He began to feel weightless, as if his body were disappearing, too, and indeed he had lost so much weight his clothing flapped on him when he walked. He began to move slowly, like an old man, to become forgetful again. His mind wandered as it used to that time at Manston Dunn. When he looked into the mirror he was surprised to see that his hair had turned completely white and his face, once so handsome, was sunken into lines and hollows. Sometimes his reflection seemed to waver and float.

He began to have thoughts about her that he'd never had before. He began to ponder their relationship, and this made him suspicious and afraid. For the first time he asked himself exactly what she had seen in him.

When they had first started to live together, he had considered himself fortunate to have acquired the love of a fine young woman. He felt he was being given another chance to reclaim his life; to mean something to someone. He vowed that this time around, he would be the perfect husband, the perfect father; instead of leaving everything to chance, letting things drift, he would let his family know he was there, play an active role, insinuate himself into their very dreams.

But now he began to look at it all from another angle. Had she perhaps seen him, a well-dressed, good-looking company executive (for he had still been an attractive man then), had she seen him as the passport to another life? Had she contrived it all, from the moment she first planted her jam jar on Miss Lindsay's desk? Why, that first time, was she so unafraid? Was it really so unexpected? She could never have foreseen then the failure he would turn out to be. Hadn't he promised to divorce his wife and marry her? He thought guiltily that he had never done so, for no reason but that in their drifting, the subject never came up. He, content with his new life, simply let it go.

She never mentioned it, but had she brooded about it? Had it made her angry?

Or, he wondered now, had that anger always been there, locked behind her innocent poses, her transparent smile, fuelling that drive which had pushed her from her country background and third-rate education to a job at Manston Dunn which no little girl like her had ever had before, which had pushed her into the arms of the son of one of the founders, into evening classes, to university, and even now – and the blood rushed to his head as he thought it – was pushing her out the door she had slammed so hard just a few minutes ago?

No, he thought, unaware that he said it out loud. For life was a blackness without her. But her hair? How could she, knowing he loved it so? But couldn't he have seen it coming? Hadn't she already divested him of everything? Wasn't it because of her that he had lost it all – his home, his wife, his children, his friends, his job, his car, his dignity? And now that she had stripped him of everything, didn't she mean to take herself away, too? He thought of her with her barbered head and saw her as someone finally exposed. Could she have sent a stronger signal? For the first time in his life he felt emotion as deep as actual pain, and he found it unbearable.

"Go!" he screamed in a voice he hardly recognized. "Go!" he shouted, as if she were there to hear. He got off the bed and stumbled to the door. "Go," he said, as if she awaited his command. When his head cleared, he was surprised to find himself on the verandah, quite alone except for her plants there, the only things in this house that flourished now. He staggered over to the plants, stood looking at them, saw them wavering, as if from a distance, filtered through an unnatural submarine light. His hands reached out. He wasn't conscious of it, it was as if another self, the one that had been lurking in the shadows all the while, had risen from the depths and taken him over, grabbed up one pot after another, smashing them down on the tiles, overturning the entire stand, beating every plant down, tearing every leaf. In a frenzy of destruction, he stomped on the bits and pieces that were left, felt wildly exultant as he looked at the battered remains, the green stains on the tiles from crushed plant juice, the smell of the damp spilled earth, the newly released earthworms.

Feeling triumphant, he staggered out to the gate. Unconscious of the shocked, wide-eyed neighbours who were gathering, he leaned both hands across it to await her return. His face and hands were bleeding where flying shards had cut him, and tiny fragments of plants and earth clung to his limbs, his clothing, his hair, as if the earth itself was sending up small signals. He held on to the gate and smiled happily, his skin a tight mask across his skull. He smiled and smiled, like a child who had done a particularly good deed and was awaiting his reward. Now she'd see that he was good at something after all.

The Chocho Vine

THE ONLY thing that flourished in Miss Evadney's yard was her chocho vine. Her son had made her sell off all the property except for the square surrounding the house, and this piece of land, neglected like her, was nothing now but hard-packed red dirt trampled by so many feet over the years, sluiced so clean by the rain and by dirty water flung from kitchen and bedroom windows, that it had acquired a shiny red patina like the ox-blood shoes her husband used to wear. By the front step, a rusting yellow margarine tin held a sickly looking Wandering Jew, and even the Ram-goat-roses which peeked out from under the house did so nervously, as if ready to jerk their heads back at the first discordant note, for though it had grown increasingly feeble in volume, Miss Evadney's temper was legendary.

The chocho vine evidently felt no fear, for in the back right-hand corner, up against the property line, it had literally captured a whole quarter of the yard, sweeping majestically over the arbour of split bamboo originally built and extended many times to hold it, clambering over the abandoned chicken coop, and then aiming upwards to almost completely smother the old Number Eleven mango tree which had after a while given up the battle and simply ceased bearing. It did put forth feeble blossoms each year on the few bits of branches which still retained the privilege of being exposed to the sun, but the tiny fruit which actually came seemed embarrassed to compete with the magnificent chochos and dried up from confusion when they were no bigger than plums. Meanwhile, the chocho vine from its high perch on the mango tree hurled itself into the air before bending down and attaching itself to a new branch, or anything else in its path, waving as if in triumph its probing tentacles and plump greeny-white offspring that were a source of unending bounty.

Miss Evadney derived great satisfaction from her splendidly robust chocho, for she was herself subject to the longest list of ailments imaginable, and any question to her about her health elicited a torrent of words, as if her infirmities, real and imagined, were now the only topic of conversation left to her. "Ai, my dear, the gas, the gas da kill me," she would commence, rubbing that part of her anatomy which was currently the locus of her pain, looking proud and surprised if she managed to produce a large belch. That greeting over, she had no trouble jumping to her "pressure," her "arthritis," her "heart," her "head," her "foot," in an endless recital which – if one didn't take care – might even include an exhibition of some afflicted part. Not that Miss Evadney had much of an audience these days since she had outlived all her contemporaries and most of the younger generation had migrated to more prosperous locations. It was really only Miss Vie and her family who paid her any mind.

Miss Vie lived up the road and had been vaguely related to Miss Evadney's husband. But that wasn't the reason why she took an interest in the old lady. The real reason was that somebody had to do it, as she often told her husband, and she saw it as her Christian duty. Besides, they were all fond of Miss Evadney, who, like so many people who tyrannized their own families and those who dared to cross them, was a perfectly benign and sociable being in her relationships with others. To them, she was almost mythical, she was so old, and could always be relied upon to give the "true version" of events whenever an argument arose or someone failed to remember things that had happened in the past. Despite her physical infirmities, Miss Evadney still had a wonderful memory.

She could remember when she had planted her first chocho vine. "It was the year I get married, Miss Vie. The said year. You see all them other girls there? All of them was busy a live common-law life. But not me, Miss Vie, not me. I had *standards*, you know." So when Mr. Shaw had the impertinence to "put question" to her, she told him she wasn't that kind of woman. "Is so I tell him," she was fond of saying, "I said, 'I am not that kind of woman. I have mother and father at my yard, so if you have anything to say, go and put question to them.'"

Mr. Shaw had just come back from the Great War, in which he had served as a volunteer. He had ten acres of land, was expecting to get his soldier's pension, and he wanted to settle down with someone. Though the white people had fixed him up in the hospital, his head still felt groggy and his chest wheezed sometimes, but he knew all this would go away once he got a good woman to look after him. He liked that Evadney Gordon, liked the cut of her jib, though he still couldn't believe this tall strapping young woman he came back to find was the skinny little pickney-gal he had left behind. That more than anything else made him conscious of how quickly time was passing, so he went to her parents and took off his hat and asked for her hand in marriage.

"Well, the other girls were so jealous afterwards!" Miss Evadney loved to say. "Here I was a married woman! And Mr. Shaw would never allow me to work again. Would never hear of his wife working. I never ever went to the ground like the other women and I never work in nobody's kitchen neither." She stayed home and looked after the house and Mr. Shaw and the three children. She kept chickens and sometimes rabbits and planted skellion and cabbages around the yard. And she planted her chocho. Mr. Shaw himself put up the arbour when the vine started to grow. Such a strong vine it was from the start.

"You have good hand with chocho," Mr. Shaw said, and she was pleased with the compliment. It was white-skin chocho, nice and fleshy inside and not too many prickles on the skin.

In those days she never sold the chochos, she gave them away, took pleasure in the fact that her vine was so bounteous she could afford to give chocho freely to all who came and asked and still have plenty left over to feed the babies on and to put in the soup or the stew. "That's the thing with chocho," she was given to saying. "It's not one of those things like pumpkin that you could get a good meal out of now. You could eat nothing but pumpkin if that was all you had and pumpkin would make yu stomach feel full. There is nothing to beat a good pumpkin soup, but chocho by itself is nothing much. Same like squash there; it's a tasteless kind of thing, you know. But to fill out the meal now, when things short, to stretch the codfish or the meat or the soup or the susumber – nothing to beat chocho."

The other good thing, Miss Evadney said, was that once you planted chocho, you didn't have to do anything but water it and give it something to climb on; the chocho would just carry on from there. Whenever her chocho vine started to look weak, she would set another one so that by the time the old one started to wear out, the young one would be flourishing.

Anyone who wanted chocho only had to come and ask; that was one rule she had. Nobody should just come into her yard and pick chocho as they liked. If they asked, they could have chocho by the dozen. But woe betide anyone who dared to take even one little vegetable without asking. Miss Evadney's tongue could blister.

When she was first married Miss Evadney wasn't at all quarrelsome. Mr. Shaw was at his ground all day and she sang as she went around doing her chores and she set his meal on the table the minute he came home. But then Mr. Shaw began to get sickly: it happened to a lot of people who had gone away to the war – "fighting for King and Country," he proudly used to say even on his sick-bed, though she was vexed that King and Country never knew anything about his coughing out his soul-case and having to take to his bed more and more. And that was the time the boys started to give trouble and back-answer her.

"Is three boy pickney I did have – Leroy, Everald, and Joseph – that is the one there we did call Mighty," she told anyone who asked. But it was only to Miss Vie or Miss Vie's daughter Hermione that she confided all. "Well, everybody know how boy pickney hard to raise from morning. And mine was no different. But you see me here, I wasn't going to let them get away with one single thing, they had to know who was boss. I let them know from morning I wasn't going to tolerate no force-ripe man at my yard. If their father couldn't chastise them anymore, they would still find out where water walk go a pumpkin belly, for I would take the strap to them myself. 'Spare the rod and spoil the child,' the Good Book says, but nobody could say I was guilty of that sin. I had *standards*, Miss Vie, *standards*. I wanted the world to know my children come from good home. All them other little pickney around could run wild and act like ragamuffin all they want. But not mine. They had to have standards, too."

When their father got too poorly to go to his ground any more, it was they who had to go. She had to take Leroy out of school before he even reached sixth standard to send him to the ground. "Leroy bawl every day because he was bright in school and had his heart set to become a teacher. Every year, every year I promise I would send him back to school, but there was no way he could go back, you almost had to say he was man-a-yard now, he had to take charge of the ground, and the two younger ones hardly ever had the chance to go to school at all for they had to help their brother. But nuh so life stay?"

Miss Evadney used to be upset about this, she often told Miss Vie: upset about the fact that her children had to drop out of school. "Because, my dear Miss Vie, if they didn't get an education, what was there for them but slaving on the land? The land wasn't a thing now that you could ever make money out of, you know. You can see for yourself that the land there never fat. Never fat. Pure hillside and rockstone. No matter how hard Mr. Shaw work, it was barely enough to keep body and soul together." Mr. Shaw's pittance from the government there, well, that was something, but it wasn't enough to send the boys to school when Mr. Shaw had to go to doctor so often and buy medicine and tonic to build up his strength. Miss Evadney remembered how she used to curse the Germans every day for what they had done to Mr. Shaw, though what it was she wasn't sure. All she knew is that they had reduced her big strapping man to nothing but a skeleton, skin and bone there lying on the bed. When the boys saw their father helpless like that, no wonder they felt they could just do as they liked.

Whenever things got too much for Miss Evadney she would go into the yard and stand and gaze in admiration at her chocho vine; it made her feel good just to look at it. One thing in her life was flourishing exuberantly. She always thought that it was a pity some of those nayga round the place were so bad-minded that they had to come and steal her chocho, were too red-eye and ill-mannered to come and ask, the way people were supposed to. Like those Pettigrews and those Vernons.

She had caught them red-handed several times and cursed them hog-rotten, them and all their generation.

When Mr. Shaw died, the pittance from the government stopped coming, and soon all the boys were gone. It was then that Miss Evadney started to sell her chocho.

"Miss Vie, I regret that I never had a daughter," she would often complain, "for I sure a daughter would stay faithful to her mother, a daughter would never, never abandon you in your old age. Daughters are always true to their mothers." Look at Miss Vie's children now, she thought to herself but didn't say out loud. Five children she has and which is the most loving to her, which one always coming to visit and bring her things? Who but the one girl pickney?

Of all Miss Vie's children, Miss Evadney loved Hermione the best. Hermione never ever came to visit her mother without bringing something for Miss Evadney. If she didn't see the old lady at her mother's, she would often walk down the road to her house, calling out loudly in jest as she neared, "Miss Evadney, Miss Evadney. Hold dog!" for Miss Evadney had not even a cat to guard her house. On these occasions, Miss Evadney felt sorry that all her neighbours had died off or moved away, sorry that they couldn't see people of quality coming to visit her at her yard.

Whenever Hermione visited her parents in the country, she always left with some of Miss Evadney's chochos. It was now a family joke: Miss Evadney and her chocho. Hermione hated the squash-like vegetables, regarding them as useless, tasteless things, and she always gave hers away. But she took the gift from Miss Evadney with many thanks, because she knew the old lady was proud to have something to give.

"Thank God for you and your mother every day, Miss H," she told her every visit, "for I don't know what I would do without you. You wouldn't believe is three boys I did birth? Three of them. Leroy the eldest, Everald the middle one, and Joseph who is the one we call Mighty for him did little but him lion-heart. And where the three of them now, eh? I ask you that. Why not a one to mind me?"

Hermione, like her mother, had heard Miss Evadney's stories so many times she didn't need to listen as the old woman talked.

"Leroy was the first one to leave home. Well I did hear some rumour there about Leroy and one of the Pettigrew girls, the one that did say she studying for nurse. But I couldn't believe it, Miss H, couldn't believe Leroy would do his mother such a thing, take up with the daughter of my enemy, those thieving red-eye people. And when I question that boy, he deny every word of it. Look straight in mi face and tell me lie, and to think how I did try to beat the lying out of them. So how I could tell anybody to this day how I did feel when my son Leroy and that girl run away together, run off to Kingston without a word to his mother?"

Miss Evadney would stand there silent for a long, long time, contemplating her fate and the injustice of it all. "Well, maybe the girl's parents did know about it, that is the hurtful part. Maybe is them fix it up to tief away my good-good boy," she would finally say in a wondering tone, as if thinking about this for the first time. "For next thing I hear, Miss H, them nuh going off to Kingston to wedding?" She even heard long afterwards that Leroy went back to school and turned teacher after all. But not a word did Leroy ever send to her, leaving her with his sick father and the ground to look after. What did she ever do to make him treat her like that?

"Miss H, I cry over Leroy, I tell you, for nothing in life never hot me so. Not even when Mr. Shaw die and leave me." She told Hermione this standing up in the middle of the road, with tears welling up in her eyes.

Mr. Shaw didn't have long to go after that disappointment and there was barely enough to bury him. "We had was to sell the three goat, though Mr. Shaw always said that because he was an old soldier the government would give something towards the burial. Well, I send and ask the government about that, and I still waiting. Thirty years now and I still waiting. You think they get the letter yet?"

The case of Everald now: Everald didn't walk off and leave her like Leroy, he just brought a woman into the house. "That didn't last long, Miss H, for though I try, God know I try, me and the girl couldn't get on, just couldn't agree." So she gave Everald permission to build his own house next door. And Everald still continued to work his father's ground and bring her something – he used to look after her, she always said, you have to give Everald that.

"But is only afterwards that I really get the full picture of what he was after, you know. For Everald is the one that make me sell off the land."

If Mighty had been around at the time, maybe she wouldn't have done it, Miss Evadney always said, but Mighty went away, too. "Mighty get to go away as farm worker, was earning good-good American dollar, turn into a fine young man, except the third time Mighty go away, he jump his contract and never come back, never send his mother another word."

So it was just she and Everald left and she was grateful to him for staying, for he looked after her and she had her grand-children next door, in and out of her house all day. And even Cynthia, their mother, and she started to pull together. So everything was working well and she could afford to just give chocho away to anybody who came and asked.

It was the bauxite coming in that caused it, Miss Evadney always maintained, that caused everything to spoil. They brought in all these machines that were digging up the earth, pulling down the mountains even, clawing away at the red dirt to ship it to America, though she always wondered why they wanted to do that, if America didn't have its own dirt. But it was the biggest thing that had happened since the war, not the war Mr. Shaw was in, the other one, and all the men around were rushing there to get work. Everald went too. He got a job working with one of these machines that was mashing down the place, and he came home beaming all over his face. The money was so good and they were going to train him and everything; he could work his way up. Everald told her that for the first time in his life, he could see his future straight like an asphalt road out there in front of him. She thought of Leroy and Mighty and felt she was going to lose Everald, too, lose him to a place where he could earn proper money and feel like a big shot, just like the others.

At first it was all right. Everald came home every weekend and went over to the ground as usual; Jackie Davison, who was his playmate from morning, and his big boy Jason were keeping an eye on things during the week. Then he started to talk of moving his family to the town where he would be nearer his workplace and Cynthia could learn to drive and shop in a supermarket and the children could go to proper schools. She knew what was coming next but this time she prayed. She prayed like she never prayed for anything else in her life, prayed that Everald wouldn't leave her, too.

Miss Evadney always said she thought it was like the devil was dealing that deck there, for look what Everald turned around and did. She was so afraid of losing him that she gave no thought to the land, said yes when he came and asked her if she would sell the land and lend him the money. "Leave only the house spot, Ma," Everald told her, "for there is no point in your keeping this land that will just go to waste when you could make something off of it now when you need it. Because I cannot keep on looking after it. My life change now. And you know once my children get education they not coming back." The way he put it, it all made sense to her, and she agreed to sell the land and let Everald borrow the money, for he needed the down payment for a house in the town. How could she stand in his way when he said she should come and live with them, there would be plenty space for her? She said, no, she could never take to life in town. So he said all right, if she stayed in her house he would look after her. He would pay back the money as soon as he could, put it into the bank to mind her in her old age.

"Where is that money now, eh?" she asked Hermione, for about the hundredth time. "Once Mister Everald get his hand on it, never see hide or hair of it again. That Everald with his sweet mouth! Is when last I see him? Tell me nuh?" Once in a while Everald would come, she reported, or his grown-up children would breeze by and leave her a little something. All driving their flashy big cars. But if she was waiting on them to live, she would starve to death.

If it wasn't for Miss Vie and Hermione, God knows what would happen to her. She was glad she had chocho to give them, for her mother always told her, "Hand wash hand. Never take something for nothing." In all her born days, she had never stooped to begging. Every Thursday Miss Mae, who higgled in the market, would come by with her little boy and a long stick and the boy would climb up and pick all the ripe chochos he could reach, and Miss Mae would pay her for them and take them to the market to sell. That was how she lived. Anyone who came by and wanted chocho now had to pay, unless she knew they were poor like her; only then she would give.

At first, when the people moved into Everald's old house next door she paid them no mind, for she was at an age where she couldn't be bothered with anything new and to her they seemed orderly and mannersable enough. Something strange was happening in the whole country these last days anyway,

Miss Evadney thought, changes were everywhere, all was topsy-turvy and confusion, it would stir up your brain to take it all in. New people were moving into the area every day. That wasn't too surprising, for all the young people had gone away; only the old people were left and the grandchildren that they had to mind.

With all the young people gone, so much of the land was idle, so many houses empty, that people from town or god-knows-where were simply coming and squatting. "Take my old land there," Miss Evadney said, "from Everald sell it to the people, they never come back once to even look at it, let it turn into wilderness, ruinate, let Everald good-good house fall to pieces, you almost have to say."

She didn't know what business these people next door had with the land and with Everald's old house, but she didn't pay them any mind at first. She heard them hammering and nail-ing, so she figured they were decent people who had come to fix up the house. "Is only when the renk ganja smell start to come from over there that I sit up straight and pay attention," she recounted later. "And more and more people were coming till I wonder how many of them planning to live in the house. Then I start to see some of those bearded fellows there, those Rastas. I never wanted any of those people living near to me. They never look good in the sight of God with their long beard and natty hair." But Miss Evadney didn't complain, for though she was too old to walk and see, people said they were clearing the whole of the land, and if they were hard-working, she said, who was she to pass judgement?

They could have got on all right, would have had no trouble

at all, no trouble, Miss Evadney always said, if they hadn't started to pick her chocho. When she saw it, she couldn't believe it, for not even when her own son was living next door would he do such a thing. These people were standing in their yard and using a long stick to cross the property boundary and hook chocho off her vine. She never raised her voice, only called out to them nicely: "Young man. Young man," she said, "is my chocho that you picking, you know?" She expected that he would say, "Sorry," and she would say, "Is all right this time, I don't mind you take a few. But next time, if you want chocho, all you have to do is ask. I only sell them at twenty cents apiece." To her amazement, though, the young man laughed when she called out to him and continued pulling down chochos. "Mother, rest yuself. You have plenty chocho to spare."

She was so shocked, she was speechless for a moment. But not for long. As soon as she recovered, she let him have the full length of her tongue. Miss Evadney thought she still had the voice she had used in the past to stun her children and frighten chocho thieves. But it had got so trembling and thin, it sounded laughably frail to the young man next door. He just continued to pick chocho. "Mother," he called out, still laughing, "you nuh hear is Socialist time now? All a we must share. Nothing nuh belong to you one any more." And before she had a chance to marshal her thoughts, hurl at him the most crushing abuse, he had picked up the chochos, *her* chocho, and disappeared into the house. Every day they came to the fence and picked chocho and got so bare-faced they did it even when they could see her standing in her yard. She would hobble over to the arbour and shout and wave her arms, but they paid her not the slightest attention, the stick continuing its remorseless passage, stabbing away at chochos until the picker decided that he had reaped enough. Each scene would leave Miss Evadney with just enough strength to make it back to her doorstep where she would sit for a while and fan herself to cool down and try to recover her composure. At first, she would go from there to Miss Vie as soon as she could manage it, to complain about the latest assault, but she did this less and less because she was shocked to discover that Miss Vie was not wholeheartedly on her side.

"Miss Evadney, I know just how you feel," Miss Vie had said. "I know it's an aggravation. But it's not like first time, you know. You have to be careful how you deal with everybody these days. Those people not good people to quarrel with, from what I hear. It would be better if you just leave them to take the chocho."

Leave them to take the chocho! Miss Vie couldn't know what she saying. It was all right for her, for she had house and land and husband and pickney and car. Could afford to give away all kind of thing. But all she had was her chocho and nobody had any right to just come and take. No right at all. She told Miss Vie as much, shaking with anger and disappointment at her attitude.

"Miss Evadney, if you want me to put it straight: you know what those people planting on the land there? I hear that is pure ganja them a plant, you know. You don't want to tangle with those kind of people."

"Plant ganja! Everybody a plant ganja these days," Miss

Evadney cried. "That is the only thing them young people farming. Them all a plant ganja. Mek them gwan. Them could plant the whole world in ganja for all I care. But that don't give them no right to take stick so pick my chocho. I bring up my boys to know right from wrong and to respect other people property. That is one thing I beat into them. Nobody could ever complain that any of my boys ever put hand on what don't belong to them. So why I should put up with other people tiefing from me?"

Miss Vie just sighed.

One day Miss Evadney came home and found some gungo peas laid out on a piece of plantain leaf on her doorstep. She cooked the gungo because she thought they were left there by one of the men around who sometimes brought her things from his ground. Another time it was a piece of pumpkin. Then one day she learned the truth. She had been home but lying down with her door shut. She'd heard a voice calling out, "Mother? Mother?" but she didn't answer because the only people who called her that were the thieving nayga boys next door. She peeked through a crack and sure enough it was one of those dirty Rastas, bending down at her doorstep. She trembled in anger. What did he want? She couldn't quite see but was satisfied that he didn't stay. She watched him leave, made sure he got off her premises without stealing anything. When she opened her door and saw a piece of yam lying there on the plantain leaf, Miss Evadney's anger knew no bounds. Did they think she was the kind of person they could just sweeten up so that she would let them take chocho as they liked? All she wanted was for them to leave her chocho alone.

She picked up the yam and plantain leaf and hobbled over to the fence where, cursing, she hurled them back into the Rastas' yard.

But Miss Evadney soon realized she would have to find other means of keeping the chocho thieves from off her vine, to let them know once and for all that she meant business. She began to keep watch on the arbour, sitting there silently hour after hour till her body got so cramped and stiff she could hardly move. When they came, she was ready for them. By her was a pile of stones which she had slowly and painfully collected. As soon as she saw the stick of the chocho thieves disturbing the foliage, she would hurl as many stones as she could over the fence, her strength so weakened that she was forced to stop and catch her breath after each throw. Though her range was short and the hail of stones ineffectual, they did cause the young men reaping the chocho to pause and even to jump to get out of range of the stronger throws. At first, they were more amused than anything and took to reasoning with her: "Lawd, Mother. Behave yuself, nuh. Why you have to fight and quarrel so with the bredren? Nuh Jah send I-bredren so help you reap Jah blessing?"

Miss Evadney simply continued with her stone-throwing. Though she never managed to hit anyone, after a while the amused cajoling turned to curses and then to threats. Once, one of them rushed to the fence with a raised machete. But still she didn't give up, screaming at the men "Unno gwine stop pick mi chocho. Even if it kill me. Not one of you ever plant chocho over here." Now they had stopped laughing, they got into the habit of shouting words across the fence even when they weren't picking chocho. And every time Miss Evadney saw them with a stick, she hurled stones.

One day, as she sat under the arbour with her pile of stones as usual, she saw the young men moving around the yard, heard them talking, heard the bad words they flung about, caught the smell of ganja on the wind. But no one came near the fence. No one attempted to pick chocho. The next day it was the same. After the third day of this she felt she had won a victory and, confident that she had finally put the chocho thieves in their place, she slept soundly for the first time in weeks. Next morning she walked as fast as her legs could take her to tell Miss Vie the good news, so pleased with herself she forgot the usual recital of her ailments. Miss Vie gave her chicken soup with chocho – her favourite – to celebrate. That night, she again slept the whole night through.

It wasn't until late the following day that she walked down to her chocho vine and immediately noticed something strange. The vine was not looking good, it seemed droopy and disheartened. She rushed to water the root, carrying the margarine tin full of water back and forth. But for all the water she poured, the chocho didn't perk up as she expected. It continued to wilt. Alarmed, she rushed over to Miss Vie and begged her to come and see what she could make of the vine, why it was drying up so.

Miss Vie came and examined the chocho carefully, looking at the arbour from various angles, disturbed at the obviously dying leaves, the colourless exposed fruit which were already shrivelling. When she could find no explanation, she went and got Miss Evadney's rickety ladder and, leaning it against the mango tree, started to climb.

"You see anything, Miss Vie?" Miss Evadney called out anxiously before she was even halfway up. With great caution, Miss Vie moved steadily up the ladder until she reached a point where she had a good view of the vine. She held on to the tree with both hands and followed the main stem with her eyes. She almost shouted out then, but caught herself just in time, for she had seen where the chocho vine had been cut, sliced right through with a sharp machete. She stood very still, gazing on the arbour, wondering how on earth she was going to find the heart to come down and tell Miss Evadney the news.

Miss Evadney, using her hand to shield her eyes against the afternoon sun so she could better see Miss Vie's every move, had spent too many years scrutinizing potential chocho thieves and wayward children to miss the quick stiffening of Miss Vie's back, the droop of her neck, her sudden stillness. In that moment of recognition, Miss Evadney audibly caught her breath and felt the stillness enter and possess her own body, emptying her of anger, of memory, of desire. Cocooned in that unaccustomed softness, she experienced only the nagging thought that, for some reason, she needed to say something to cheer up Miss Vie, to get her down safely from the ladder. "Well, the thing about chocho now," Miss Evadney heard herself saying, "the thing about chocho now," she said again and kept on saying long after Miss Vie had climbed back down the ladder to find her trembling and wordless.

Zig-Zag

THE QUEENDOM of Hyacinths was located in and around
the granadilla arbour where at one point in their lives they
spent a lot of their time together, dressed up in their mother's
clothes and acting out their fantasies, that time before a real
princess ascended the throne, before Muffet went away to
school, before Sadie and Manuela mashed up the playhouse,
imprinted it with so much squalor nobody ever used it again.
Not that they discussed it or came to any decision about it,
that's just how it turned out. Muffet began to spend a lot more
time with her books and Manuela never came to play with
them again.

That left just Sadie knocking around the place, getting in
people's way and asking questions and faasing in everything,
annoying Mother Dear and Desrine by turns till they would
shout at her to go away and find something to do. Sadie was a
restless spirit.

155

"As if mad-ants just biting her all the time," Desrine complained. "Never see a chile restless so."

I am just like Manuela, Sadie thought, but she didn't say it aloud, for Desrine was Manuela's mother and if she didn't know that, who did?

Although Sadie was still carrying bad feelings in her heart for that Manuela, she was still sorry she hadn't yet come this summer, because – she couldn't tell a lie there – she had really liked that girl. Manuela liked her, too, or so it seemed, before she got to know Muffet. In that respect Manuela had turned out to be like everyone else, was no different from those society people Mother Dear took tea with, for it looked as if they didn't like Sadie much either. Not half as much as they liked Muffet, though whenever Sadie brought up the subject with Mother Dear, she said don't be so thin-skinned and sensitive.

It was all right for Mother Dear to talk like that, everyone knew where she was coming from: she was a Ferguson, of the Portland Fergusons, Papa's father had been the Reverend Chance, and though she and Papa didn't have money – she was always joking about that – they came from Somewhere. And if they did, so did Sadie.

"You come from Somewhere, Sadie, from Good Family, make no mistake about it," Mother Dear was always saying. "You can hold your head up high."

Muffet knew how to walk with her head held high, all right. Knew exactly where she was coming from and where she was going. Which is why, before Manuela started to come regularly for the summer holidays, they had this Queendom of Hyacinths which was full of nice high-class people. The Lady this and the Lady that, the Duke and the Duchess, and such types.

At first, Sadie was pleased with the name because the blue water hyacinths which floated in the pond were her favourite flowers, but then she discovered that those weren't what Muffet had in mind. Once when she referred to this, Muffet said witheringly, "I'm talking about *proper* flowers, Sadie, not weeds."

"Weeds!" Sadie shrieked, as she did about anything that offended her, causing those around her with soft voices to wince with embarrassment.

After Muffet had paused long enough to register her disapproval of Sadie's loud, common voice, she said: "Those things are weeds, you know that. A terrible pest. Why do you think they try to kill them every year? Real hyacinths are proper flowers. They grow in *England*. People go gathering them in meadows."

"What's 'meadows'?" Sadie asked.

"Pastures," said Muffet.

"So why can't they gather them in the pastures?"

"Because pastures are full of ticks and cow dung and cows. And meadows are full of hyacinths and daffodils and written about in books."

Sadie wanted them to call it the Kingdom of Granadillas to celebrate the large green-skinned passion-fruit which hung over their heads like arboreal melons and yielded pulp of an unbearable sweetness, but Muffet said no, they had to choose a foreign name. Why? asked Sadie. Because foreign is elegant and written about in books, said Muffet. Who ever heard of granadilla? I have! Sadie shouted. But Muffet was adamant, and

Muffet, being the eldest, usually ended up getting her own way because Sadie got bored easily with arguing and told herself she had better things to do with her time. Sometimes she really couldn't think of anything better, so she would suddenly jump up and kick pupalick. As she turned cartwheels her dress would fly over her head exposing her baggy and Muffet would shriek "Sadie!" and her face would turn bright red. Muffet was always turning red.

Sometimes Sadie would shinny up the huge mango tree against which the granadilla arbour was built and, wrapping her feet around a limb, would poke her head through the foliage of the arbour, her face framed by her wild untidy hair suddenly appearing upside-down among the plump granadillas. Muffet would glare at her and move out of range because she was terrified of lizards dropping. Sadie would laugh and, righting herself, would swing a foot down through the leaves. "Heh-heh-hey," she would cackle, as loud and careless as a marketwoman.

Muffet would roll her eyes to heaven indicating that Sadie was being A Trial. Mother Dear was always shaking her head and saying so, for as long as they could remember, and Muffet was beginning to find her A Trial, too.

"Sadie, are you playing this game or not?" she would ask sharply.

"Okay," Sadie would say, dropping to the ground. "What's a 'queendom'?"

"It's a country ruled over by a queen."

"Who's the queen?"

"Me."

"Who's the king?"

"There's no king."

"It must have a king."

"Who says?"

"Everybody says. King and queen. They go together."

"Oh yes? Who's 'everybody'?"

"Papa and Mother Dear."

"Go and ask them. They'll tell you you don't have to have kings."

"Ray Delvallie could be king," Sadie said, and Muffet glared at her, for Ray Delvallie was the baddest boy around, so bad that Mother Dear had forbidden them even to speak his name.

"Sadie, don't be stupid," Muffet said. "I am the queen. You can be the queen's lady-in-waiting."

"I don't want to be a lady-in-waiting. Why should I be a lady-in-waiting? I want to be a princess."

"You can't."

"Why not?"

"Because queens and princesses have good hair."

"You damn, rotten liar!"

"Sadie!" Muffet hissed.

When Sadie had quietened down, Muffet said in a voice of great reasonableness, "It's true. It's all in the books. Long, straight hair. Have you ever seen a princess with a natty head?"

"I don't want to play this stupid game, then," Sadie said, flinging herself on the ground and behaving as if she didn't care, but she could feel her heart tightening against her chest for she knew what Muffet said was true.

"Okay," Muffet said in a conciliatory tone, for she couldn't play the game alone. "You can pretend to be a princess. I'll let you be a princess. A princess in the Queendom of Hyacinths."

"Queendom of Hyacinths," Sadie repeated, liking the way it sounded, instantly becoming a princess.

Their play-acting sometimes lasted all afternoon. From the time they finished their homework till Desrine called them in for supper, and often on weekends and holidays, they lived in their imaginary queendom.

Sometimes, though, Sadie got tired of being a princess and all the pretending, of the speaky-spokey life it entailed, for Muffet said princesses had to speak properly at all times. So she would go and hang around Desrine in the kitchen, its entrance looking dark and sooty like the bat-infested caves in the hills. The walls and ceiling were black from the smoke of the imperfectly vented fireplace Desrine used for roasting breadfruit, cooking dogfood, and boiling water for baths in the ten-gallon tin which she would heave onto her head and carry across the back yard to the house.

If Sadie didn't find Desrine in her lair, she would go to the Calidonia Dover wood-burning stove, which was Desrine's pride, and lift up the heavy pot lids and peep inside, savouring the aroma of Desrine's cooking, look inside the oven to see if anything was baking, play with Desrine's tea bush, herbs and spices hanging on the wall or tied up in little bundles or stuffed into old tins on the shelves, which she'd take down and open to inhale their sweetness, their pungency, and crush pieces between her fingers to extract their promise: rosemary, thyme, pimento, cerassie, fever grass, and see-me-contract. She would poke about in dark corners to examine the brown dried sarsa-parilla, the cinnamon sticks, the mounds of round nutmegs in their shells, yellow ginger root, sorrel the colour of ox-blood. The only fresh things were whatever bush teas and seasonings Desrine picked around the yard that day and the bright pink kola nuts which she kept on hand as antidote for poison and also grated for her tea every morning, for everybody knew bisi was the very thing to keep down pressure and cure bad feelings.

"Don't ask if Desrine don't know about bush and thing," Sadie was always boasting to her classmates. "The minute you get fever, Desrine know what to do. Is her mother Miss Mary she get it from. Miss Mary get it from her ol'grandfather, who was a true-true African." She always tried to make that sound as mysterious as possible.

Sadie liked to have things like that to talk about, for she knew her boldness shocked the girls she was supposed to mix with at school. None of them would dream of admitting they knew anything about bush and Africans, for they were busily preparing to go to high school where their fathers would pay large fees so they could be turned into ladies who would straighten their hair and rub Ponds Vanishing Cream into their faces every night and wear 4711 toilet water and learn to squeeze their bodies into corsets and their feet into tiny shoes so they would have bunions for the rest of their lives. All the real ladies Sadie knew – like Mother Dear and her friends – had bunions, and she assumed it was a badge that came from their having attended The Best Schools, an accomplishment they were always boasting about, like coming from Good Family. So what a thing if they ever heard Sadie with this African business! Real autoclaps! as Desrine would say. Worse if any of them saw who Sadie mixed with round the corner at recess time, playing marbles with the boys, even. Children who came shoeless to school and smoked cigarettes made from any old dried bush (unless they could snatch a tobacco leaf or two hanging out to dry) and who never washed behind their ears; wutless, scabby, natty-head children who would say and do anything, for everybody knew they had no shame and were going nowhere, according to Desrine. Desrine always deplored the condition of those children as they passed by to and from school, dirty, yelling, and unkempt. She acted as if they were a personal affront and cursed their parents for being bungo. Bungo people had no ambition. Nobody could accuse Desrine of being bungo; ambition for her children was all she had, even if so far (it always grieved her to say it) she hadn't yet succeeded in buying any of them shoes.

"Sadie!" Desrine would yell the minute she came into the kitchen and found Sadie there messing about with her things. "What you doing in here? You turn Kitchen Bessie? Why you don't go out and play like them other one? What you come in here for to bother me today?"

Desrine would go stomping around, banging pots and pans and opening cupboard doors and pulling out drawers just so she could slam them shut and generally act as vexed as could be. Desrine was like a coil there, man, like a snake, ready to spring if you just say, "Fe!" But Sadie paid her bad temper no mind.

"What you making, Desrine?" she would ask, already pouring flour carefully into the measuring cup and from there into the big sifter she had placed over the cream mixing bowl. "One cup? Two cups? How many cups you want, Desrine? Salt? A teaspoon?"

Desrine would forget herself enough to say, "Two. Yes. Cut in the lard." Before she even realized what she was doing, she would be supervising Sadie making the pie. Or else Sadie would grab up the vegetables and start peeling. Chop up the skellion. Slice the onions. Using the sharp kitchen knife she knew she wasn't supposed to use.

"Sadie!" Desrine would say, but in a nicer voice.

While Sadie worked – or watched as the case might be – she cross-examined Desrine about all manner of things, because if anybody liked to know people's business – so her sister Muffet said – it was Sadie. Since Manuela's last visit, there had been only one thing on Sadie's mind.

"So, Desrine, Manuela not coming to stay again?" She had been asking that question for almost a year now. Not that Sadie wanted to be reminded of Manuela, but the subject was irresistible, like using your tongue to play constantly with a loose tooth.

Manuela was Desrine's big daughter who – like her other six children – lived with her mother Miss Mary and her father Mass Eustace in a district called Mount Hebron, which was deep in the bush many miles away.

Sadie remembered the time she had accompanied Desrine on one of her trips home, the first time she herself had left home without any of her family, and how big and important it made her feel to come back and talk about it.

"No road there at all. No bus or buggy or truck or even a bicycle could get up there. No sir," Sadie was always informing her sister or her friends, "not an easy place to find." She instructed them, as if they would ever want to go to a place so remote: "You take the *Confidence* bus as far as Tom Johnson Corner on the main road, where that big cotton tree is, just past Baptist Church? That's where you get off. Then you follow the track which crosses the river and zig-zags up and around the mountains. You walk and walk, looking down at the precipice and up at the huge poinciana and breadfruit and flame-of-the-forest trees – nothing grows small up there, no sir, it's like real jungle – every kind of tree spreading over the road so it's cool and shaded all the way and damp, which is why the ferns and begonias and ginger lilies covering the banks have a perky look as if they've just been bathed and not dried off yet."

Sadie would pause to see the effect her story was having, but would continue regardless: "There is so much to see on the way to Desrine's yard," she would say (though Muffet never believed her for she didn't like Desrine), "what with looking down at the houses far below and up at the mountains far above wondering how you're ever going to get over. The people zig-zagging follow-line down the track all know Desrine and greet her nicely for the track's so narrow everyone has to stop to give pass. Oh yes" – she nods to Muffet's sceptical stare – "everyone gives pass to Desrine for they know she is Miss Mary one-daughter working out in Big-People house, so plenty respect for Desrine. You should see how they treat Desrine in those parts, girl. Like she's Big-People herself." Now Muffet rolls her eyes, certain that Sadie's making it up, but Sadie pays no attention to her lack of enthusiasm and continues her recital:

"Of course Desrine's children, Jason Sam Manuela Mikey Robert JunieBird and BabyErrol waiting by the roadside to greet her before she even gets off the bus. Before Co'Nizac draw brake good to stop *Confidence*, they jumping up and down by the roadside screaming, 'Mama come! Mama come!' and grabbing all the things Shadrack the sideman handing down from the tailgate and Desrine passing over the side" (for everyone knows *Confidence* in truth is really just a truck, a truck with planks for benches). Sadie is getting into high gear now: "They passing down the shutpan with cooked food and the margarine box with store-bought groceries and the other big box that the radio came in just the other day but Papa said Desrine could have it for he really likes Desrine and he doesn't want her to leave no matter what anybody says for Desrine never ever touches his papers and that box is full of outgrow clothes that Mother Dear gave to Desrine." Sadie pauses to stare at Muffet at that point, expecting her to make some rude comment about Desrine, but she seems to be paying not the slightest attention. Sadie is not the least bit deterred; she barrels on, since her stories have the habit of assuming a momentum of their own. "From they scream out, 'Mama come!' the children, except for Manuela, never say another word, they so tongue-tied, but you can see their bodies straining with excitement till they almost flying off the ground, their eyes bug-out and shining like peenie. They rush around like mad-ants and grab up all the parcels and boxes and put them on their heads and run off up the track. There's nothing for Desrine to carry but her changepurse and her handkerchief which she carries down her bosom anyway, so her hands are free for taking

BabyErrol from Manuela. But see here! She's hugging and kissing him up so much JunieBird, the next in size, who is on her brother Jason's shoulder and looking back, gets jealous and starts to cry, bawling out, 'Mama!' with her arms outstretched. So Desrine shouts to one of the bigger ones to stop and hands Errol over and takes JunieBird in her arms and carries her and hugs her and kisses her too till the next one Robert starts hanging on to her skirt tail and pulling. So she shouts to one of the bigger ones to stop and she hands JunieBird over and bends down and hugs up Robert for he's too big to be carried and she and Robert walk hand in hand for a while. Till you see the one name Mikey? The one carrying on like he's too big for all that sort of thing? The first one to run off? Well, this same Mikey starts to hang back, hang back till he's right by his mother's side and he rubs up against her. Oh my! Such an accident! So she reaches her hand out and places it on his head and draws him to her and Mikey shyly reaches out his hand and puts it around her waist and the two of them so tight, walking up the hillside. Then Jason and Sam! The two big ones? The ones behaving as if they turn man already? Ducking and laughing when their mother's trying to hug them? Well, mi dear, what you think happen?" Again Sadie appeals to the silent Muffet. Again she rushes on: "At night when she's there lying on the big bed that they make with two flourbag mattresses stuffed with cornhusk on the floor and all of them crowding in around her, fighting to get close to her, who are the very ones lying right next to her, right under her armpit, you have to say? Eh?"

Sadie could give Muffet all this information because one

weekend Mother Dear had finally given in after months – no, years – of pleading and allowed her to go with Desrine to her house in the bush and she had walked zig-zag up the hill behind everyone else, hand in hand with Desrine's big daughter Manuela, who held on to her the minute she stepped off the bus.

Sadie knew barefoot Manuela was showing off walking with her like that, showing her off to all the people they passed, grown-ups as well as Manuela's schoolmates who were jealous that Manuela had backra pickney with long hair and ribbons and starched pretty dress and hat and shoes and socks to walk hand in hand with. The children just stood and stared at them, running back up the hill after they passed out of sight so they could continue to stare. Manuela spoke nicely to the grown-ups they passed, very nicely, for duppy know who to frighten, but she never spoke to the people her own age, she just held on to Sadie and stuck her nose in the air and pretended she didn't see them, knowing full well she was making them mad with jealousy. But Manuela wasn't going to admit she knew those ragamuffin children while Sadie was there. Monday morning, she'd go to school and the bolder ones would malice her off for being bad-minded and poor-show-great just because she had backra pickney at her yard. But after a while their curiosity would overcome their hostility so Manuela would just wait and not say a word, and by lunch break they would come crowding around asking questions and she wouldn't tell them a thing until they had given her some of their cut-cake or their cane or a paradise plum or whatever food they had. She couldn't help it if those children were all so ignorant and foolish they didn't have mother working in Big-People house and so have plenty things to talk about.

Manuela explained all this to Sadie as they walked slowly up the hill, arm in arm, how those children were so faas and behaved as if they were the worst kind of cuffee come from Mocho and not worth talking to.

"Is so black people stay, you know, Sadie. Them don't have no mind. You see like how me don't even notice them? Is them same one a come crowd round me Monday morning so ask me question."

With the thought of her tales being retailed all over Manuela's school, with surefooted Manuela to hold on to, with so many people to call out greetings to on the track and in the houses they passed, Sadie found that in no time at all they had flown up the hill to Miss Mary and Mass Eustace's house perched on the hillside. Sadie and Manuela were the last ones to come up, by which time the rest of them were standing there laughing, watching them zig-zagging up the hill, shouting encouragement to Sadie as if it were a race (and Sadie well-tired by this time, in truth, as she always said), calling out until they left the main track and cut onto the path which led to the yard where Desrine and her family waited.

Except for Manuela, Desrine's children all had black shiny skin like hers and hair that was short and coarse. "Natty head," Manuela called them all. "Bungo pickney." To their faces. Manuela was several shades lighter than the other children, with big round eyes framed with delicate half-moon eyebrows and purplish skin like a starapple, and she had a much straighter nose, a proper nose which she got from her grandmother, she proudly told Sadie, not Miss Mary, who was black and had a flat nose like the rest of them, but her father's mother who was born in Panama and had Indian blood in her – so her father had told Desrine, a Panama lady that he named his first daughter after.

Because Manuela had come out with cool skin and hair that was longer and softer than the others', everybody treated her as if she were someone special, even Desrine, Sadie could see that. That weekend Desrine had spent hours rubbing bleaching cream into Manuela's skin to make it lighter and softer. She also had all sorts of pomades and miracle creams she bought from the Syrian pedlar and took home on each visit to rub into Manuela's hair to make it grow. Sadie was surprised to hear Desrine say she would get Manuela's hair straightened as soon as she left school, for one of the things Sadie knew Desrine felt bad about was that she couldn't afford to get her own hair straightened like the other women who worked for the Big-People – Irene and Cherry and Clarissa – who went to Destiny's Hairdressing Parlour at the back of Tailor shop for their hot comb every Saturday afternoon. "Oh Sadie, I feel so shame," Desrine often said, shame that she had to go home and greet her children not with hair straightened but done up in little plaits hidden by her head-tie, with her brown felt hat, which she always wore when travelling, jammed down tight on top. "But I can't do better ya, for water more than flour," she'd say. "Have to wait till the children grow big and can manage before I look after myself, man." Desrine also declared, in her more optimistic moments, "My day will come, for what is fe you can't be un-fe you."

Sadie used to feel for Desrine, for in truth those other women who worked in the Big-People house, Irene and Cherry and Clarissa, oh, they looked sharp as razors on their days off. Stylish as anything. The sweet scent of Khus Khus licking hot when they passed by the side of the house to go around the back to visit with Desrine.

"I just drop by since I passing, Desrine, drop by to see how you doing, girl." That's what they all said, every one, don't think Sadie wasn't noticing, and it was dropping by in truth for they never stayed long, just long enough to su-su a little and show off on Desrine. That little Cherry with her wire-waist drawn in tight with a broad belt. That Clarissa who came dressed to back foot in an elaborate new outfit every time for her mistress Mrs. Delvallie was always throwing things her way. So Clarissa would be dressed in satin and lace and frills and beading and sequins and furs and feathers, walking up and down in the sun so hot rivulets of sweat would run down the white powder caked on her face. She looked as if she herself would just melt away encased in all her finery, melt and leave the clothing to walk on down the road by itself, so stiff with sequins and draping and all, but she didn't complain for she had to show her dresses off. Then there was brown, slow-moving Irene behaving like a lady herself with her cool skin and her clothes that was nobody's cast-off, she made sure everybody knew that (especially if her friend Clarissa was around). All of these women coming by to show off on Desrine. When they left, Desrine's mouth would long out worse than ever. Sadie knew Desrine had only one pair of shoes and one hat and one good dress which she wore every time she went home and which was patched under the arms and she didn't want her shoes to spoil so the minute she got off *Confidence* and left the main road and turned up the track, she took off the shoes and buckled the straps together and hung them round her neck so people could see that although she was walking barefoot, she was somebody that had shoes.

So the day when Sadie visited at Desrine's yard, she was amazed to hear her promising to straighten Manuela's hair, Manuela who hadn't even reached fourth standard in school yet. Desrine had been sitting barefoot on the bench under the almond tree and Manuela was sitting on the ground between her mother's legs with her head back while Desrine rubbed miracle cream from a big jar into Manuela's hair. The other children were looking on and that Manuela was just sitting there, looking pleased as any puss.

During the school holidays, for as long as Sadie could remember, one or another of Desrine's bigger boys always came to spend time with her. But after Sadie's visit to them, it was Manuela who came each time, for Desrine said Manuela was old enough now to help in the house. Not that she wanted Manuela to do domestic work, she explained, Manuela was too good for that, but every girl child should learn to keep house and do things for themselves. Besides, she said, girl children needed more attention, and that Manuela was getting big. At first, Sadie could discern no sign of bigness in Manuela, who was as skinny as Muffet though, at eleven, she was a year older. By the next year, though, she had shot up several inches. And last year, the last time she came, they were astonished to see that she had grown breasts and hips like a woman, for she was bursting out of her clothes. The minute she arrived, Mother Dear took one look and sent Muffet and Sadie down to Mr. Chin to buy yards of cambric and rushed to her sewing machine so the child could be "decently clad," she told Desrine. Mother Dear would not allow Manuela to leave the yard until she could be enveloped in dresses which made her look not quite so much like a ripe juicy starapple ready to burst out of its skin.

At first when Manuela started to come to Sadie's house, she was nothing like the girl Sadie had met. Her true-true nature revealed itself slowly. She didn't preen as she had done at her own house. Unless she was alone with Sadie, she didn't speak unless she was spoken to, and even then she hung her head and mumbled. Manuela after all was Desrine's daughter, and Desrine made sure she never forgot her place. If Manuela once stepped out of bounds, say she was playing with the girls and she laughed too loud, her mother would pull her up sharply. All Desrine had to do was push her head out of a window and say, "Eh, Miss," and Manuela would clap her hands to her mouth for forgetting herself. If she did forget herself while Desrine was near, Desrine's hand would flash out like lightning and, without even looking, she'd give Manuela a good quick slap, for Desrine never make joke with her children. Never make joke to chastise them when they're wrong. So she always said. Sadie would feel for Manuela, who would jump at the blow, more with shock at the suddenness of it than anything else, and rub wherever it was that the lick fell. But she would never cry, not even when Desrine caught her a good clip on the side of her head.

At the start of Manuela's visit each year, Sadie would watch her but would not act like her friend, she would wait for Muffet to act first. Sadie could not explain it but she had the feeling she had to watch herself, had to be careful how she played with Desrine's daughter, for Sadie was the one in the family at some kind of risk, everybody knew that, at risk of "turning down." Hadn't she heard her Aunt Mim say that, with her own two ears?

But Muffet would end up playing with Manuela though she, too, made sure Manuela never forgot her place. If Manuela once forgot herself and acted too familiar, Muffet wouldn't hesitate to give her a withering stare, or cut her dead, and she'd end the playing right there. At those times, Sadie always found herself feeling confused, never knowing whether to take up for Manuela or side with Muffet. Usually she did neither, she just pretended she couldn't be bothered to concern herself with any of it. But she really liked to be around Manuela, for outside the house and out of earshot of their mothers, Manuela came alive and showed her true self. Sadie liked to challenge her. Jacks and skipping and hopscotch. Manuela always won. She brought some rude rhymes from her school, too (which she told only to Sadie):

Rain a fall, breeze a blow
Chicken batty outa door.

And rude behaviour. When they played Brown Girl in the Ring and it was Manuela's turn to "show her motion," Muffet was shocked by her movements as she lifted her skirt and gyrated her hips. Next time Sadie was in the ring, she felt she had to raise her skirt even higher than Manuela's and move her hips wildly, too. Muffet wouldn't let them play Brown Girl in the Ring for the rest of the summer.

Once Muffet accepted Manuela as a playmate, Sadie felt proud then to have her as a friend; proud that she knew Manuela better than Muffet did, that she had spent time at her house. Last summer, up to a certain point in time, until Manuela made Sadie do such a terrible thing there, something Sadie didn't even want to think about, they seemed to have spent a lot of time arm in arm. Sadie was embarrassed whenever she thought about it, for she could never forget the look of scorn on Muffet's face that day down in the arbour. Sadie had kept far from Manuela after that, neither of them played with her again, and Manuela seemed to spend all of her time helping her mother. Sadie tried her best not to notice Manuela as she carried water on her head from the tank to the bathroom. Hung out the clothes she helped her mother wash. Got down on her hands and knees to polish the floor. Tried her best not to notice her, though how could she help it when that girl just took over all Sadie's thoughts as if she were living right there inside Sadie's head even when she was nowhere in sight?

Manuela certainly had ruined the last summer holidays for

Sadie, who had taken to wishing with all her heart that Manuela would leave. Her presence had made Sadie nervous and prickly. Guilty. Of what, precisely, she wasn't sure.

All this summer, whenever Desrine went home, Sadie waited with some apprehension for her to return with Manuela in tow. But week after week, Sadie spied Desrine coming up the road alone. Every time, she stood by the gate waiting for Desrine zig-zagging between elation and despair.

— —

Now, sitting in Desrine's kitchen helping to shell the freshly picked broad beans for the oxtail stew Desrine was preparing, Sadie tried again to find out about Manuela. She liked it when Desrine decided to cook complicated dishes, for she then had to pay more attention than usual to what she was doing and this caused things she wouldn't normally tell Sadie to just fly out of her mouth. Sadie sat there watching Desrine taking pieces of oxtail from the yabba where they had been soaking in the seasoning, and putting them to brown in the big black Dutch pot where hot oil was already sizzling. Desrine was silent for a while, seemingly intent on her work, then she suddenly paused and, stabbing the air with the big three-pronged fork she held in her right hand to accentuate her words, she came out with: "There's a limit to what poor parents can manage, when water more than flour."

Sadie nodded, settling down to a good listen, for she knew Desrine was referring to her children's education, one of her favourite topics.

"The thing is, Sadie," she said, "the thing is that Missis Queen, the Queen of England that was? The one that decide these things long long ago from slavery done?" Sadie nodded, for she'd heard this many times before. "From she say yes, nayga people can go free, Missis Queen say, well now, she would be willing to provide a school place if you want, till that child reach a certain age, yes, but she never say one living thing about doing anything after that. When that time finish is you the parents have to find money for the schooling, pupil teacher or even reach to high school which is where you and your sister going. Backra pickney can stay in school for them parents can afford it. Stay as long as they like. Till them all grow beard. But is not so for black people."

Desrine stabbed at a piece of meat with the fork and took it out of the pot, then she held it in the air as she thought for a moment before laying it on the brown paper to drain. "Well, me can't quarrel with King or Queen as the case may be, for is clear a England them live so them can't know how hard nayga have to work out them soul-case so find food for the pickney here, much less find school fee. Clear slap a England, you nuh see it, Sadie? Bucknam Palace. So how them must know what a gwan here? Governor na send and tell them. Governor na send and tell them one living thing. You nuh see it?"

Sadie nodded and felt her interest grow. She knew Desrine was getting to the subject of Manuela. Last summer, Manuela, who had turned thirteen, had just finished elementary school. Desrine had decided to pay the headmaster to give her extra lessons, so she could stay in school a little longer, for (said

Desrine) that is what all ambitious parents did. But now, here was Desrine saying she wasn't sure Manuela was cut out for studying, no matter how much bath she got to strengthen her brain, how much oil to fix her head on her shoulders good.

"Is not little bush Miss Mary use on that Manuela there," Desrine said, almost to herself. "Plenty candle burn. Plenty fish head boil even when them other one don't get, for them don't need brain food yet." And plenty *guzu* make for Manuela to wear under her clothes, Sadie thought, but she didn't say it aloud, for Manuela had once told Sadie that her *guzu* – the packet on the red string she wore around her neck to keep duppy away – was secret-secret thing that not even Sadie suppose to ask about and Sadie would die and turn into Rolling Calf if she ever breathed a word, especially to her mother, Miss Vivi, who would fly at Manuela to throw away them heathenish thing. Shout at Manuela with vexation and shame her as she did that time when she ordered Manuela to undress so she could try on the clothes she was making, and Manuela nearly died with fright for she never had time to hide her *guzu* before Miss Vivi caught sight of it and tore it off and flung it through the window in dire vexation.

"Miss Vivi never know how much harm she could do that day, she mussa never know," Manuela told Sadie afterwards, "for she not a wicked lady. But, Sadie, from that moment till your mother finish with me and I dash outside and pick up mi *guzu* and put it on again (thank God it never burst), I swear mi heart stop beating. Yes, is like mi rightful self did leave me gone. I nearly dead with fright. Only Massa God know how duppy never tek me over when Miss Vivi do such a wicked thing, ask pardon, throw weh mi *guzu* and leave me naked and unprotected like the day a born."

Listening to Desrine talk about educating Manuela, Sadie wondered why they bothered since nothing seemed to make Manuela a good student. Manuela herself had often said she didn't care for books at all. Sadie knew Desrine wanted Manuela to become somebody and learn a trade — Manuela had had her heart set on hairdressing. But now, it sounded like Desrine herself was beginning to despair. Sadie watched as she picked up a pinch of salt and threw it in a pot of water boiling away at the back of the stove.

"It look like Manuela too flighty, if you know what a person mean," Desrine said. Sadie looked up from the peas she was shelling but said nothing. "No matter how hard you try, ya Sadie, if you squeeze scissors, you can't get oil. You can't get honey from gourd. You can't get blood out of stone."

Sadie nodded her head in agreement. Even she knew that.

"Nuh bother think bout put yuself in barrel if matchbox can hold you, ya," Desrine warned. "If is domestic work you cut out to do, that is what you cut out to do. Basket can't carry water. I have ambition for Manuela, plenty ambition. But if her brain can't take the studying, if it stay like strainer, it just have to leave to Massa God."

Desrine fell silent for a good long while. Then she burst out with: "Not a thing wrong with domestic work, if it come to that. Look at me here, Sadie, look at me. Barely thirteen when I start work out. And look at me now. If me never learn domestic work from before me start have pickney, is how I would mind them all now? Me one?"

Sadie looked at Desrine as she commanded, looked at her closely as she stood by the stove, her face beaded with sweat, but she wasn't sure what she was supposed to see. She didn't expect to compare Desrine to Mother Dear, or to Mrs. Turner or Mrs. Delvallie or any of those rich ladies. They were real ladies who wore pretty clothes and hats and had lovely hands and smelled beautiful all the time and drank tea out of china cups and had people like Desrine to do their work. The Turners, who owned most of the land around, had not one maid as they did, but about three maids in all and a gardener and somebody to look after the horses and everything, not counting all the men and women who worked as labourers on their estate. Rich people. The women all looked pretty and had good hair. Of course, Mother Dear looked like that, too, looked as good as any of them, for Mother Dear came from Somewhere, never mind they had no money. Mother Dear was always saying so, for, she said, she didn't want her daughters to grow up having false illusions.

"My girls will have to be twice as good as everybody else," she was fond of telling them at bedtime when she came into their room and sat on their beds and heard their prayers. "My girls will have to be twice as well-mannered and pretty and bright as those others. Remember, dears, unlike them, you have no great inheritance to expect, not any more. You simply must make the best of what you have, so you too can go forth and shine." She always said this with a dramatic flourish as if to will it so.

Sadie didn't know how she was going to shine, but she knew what Mother Dear meant about their not being rich because she could see their house wasn't as splendid as those of the people Mother Dear liked to mix with. Yet she was secretly glad that they didn't have to live in a grand house like the Turners or the Richardses or the Delvallies did, a grand house set on top of a hill with a long, long driveway and painted every year. She liked their house all right, liked how pretty it looked from the road with the sloping double roof of many different weathered shingles showing where it was patched each time and the whitewashed Spanish walling, the green-painted jalousies and shutters and the white fretwork, the way as you approached it from the road you could see only the upper part of the house through the thick hibiscus hedge that Mother Dear made the yardboy keep so neat with his machete. Then you got to the wooden gate and walked down the short curving driveway outlined in big whitewashed rocks with the stately royal palms on one side, almost dwarfing the bungalow.

At one corner of the front verandah was an exuberant red bougainvillea clawing its way right to the housetop and, on the other side, a clump of sedate fan palms turning their leaves down as if they were shamed by the brazen bougainvillea. Sadie loved that bougainvillea. The front verandah itself was cool and shaded with Mother Dear's palms and geraniums in plump clay pots on wrought-iron stands and green-painted deep wooden verandah chairs that you could sink into and get lost in. Sadie preferred their house to any other. Though Muffet would rather live in a grand house like the Turners. She constantly criticized their own house because the whitewash was flaking from the walls, the paint on the doors and window frames was cracked and fell off in bits, the wicker on the furniture was uncoiling itself, and the colour was leaching out of the cushions day by day.

Sadie never noticed any of these things though Mother Dear pointed them out, too. Pointed them out to Papa on a Sunday afternoon when they sat on the verandah and she listed all the things she planned to have looked after as soon as the pimento money was in. Or they sold the heifer. Or the oranges. Or some other thing. Mother Dear had these schemes, but by the time the money came, there were shoes to buy or taxes to pay. The grocer's and doctor's bills to meet. Things to be done to take shame out of their eyes.

Shame was always in Muffet's eyes. "Shame-Brown-Lady, Shamey-Shamey-Lady," Sadie called her when she wanted to tease, for she thought her sister was just like the mimosa plant in the pasture that slammed its leaves shut at the slightest touch, even by a breath of wind, in order to bare its prickles to the world.

"That's because you have no shame at all. You're shameless. You're never going to amount to anything," Muffet would retort.

Sadie laughed her cackling laugh and acted shameless as the bougainvillea. "Ha-ha, Shamey-lady," she sang out. But tears pricked her eyes, for suppose what Muffet said was true? That she would never amount to anything. It was entirely possible, for she knew she was the one destined to turn down. Hadn't she overheard Aunt Mim saying so the last time she visited? "When blood gets mixed, Vivi," said Aunt Mim, whose face was as pale as Excelsior water crackers, "you have to make sure the right blood wins out. A-oh. You just watch that little Sadie there, for she could easily *turn down*. It's unfortunate but true; she takes after the *other side*." For the listening Sadie, the words, half-whispered, were bursting with meaning, overflowing with dread.

"You know Mother Chance was an extremely cultured woman – her whole family – never mind they were dark – you could never deny that, Mim," Mother Dear said in a tight voice, as if straining the words with her teeth (for she always tried hard to keep on the right side of her older sister). "I don't see why you are saying things like –"

Sadie, whose ears were burning, was destined to hear no more, for Desrine came round the side of the house and caught her standing right by the verandah. "Listening as usual to things that don't concern you, eh, Miss," she hissed as she rushed over and hauled her off.

"But is my business they talking. Do, Desrine," she cried, "I beg you. I just want to hear a little thing there."

"Pickney can't have business, Miss. Don't be impertinent," Desrine told her. "Cockroach have no business inna fowl roos."

Try as she might, Sadie was never able to overhear any of this matter again, but she had heard enough, for she suddenly knew what Aunt Mim meant. Looking at the family with newly opened eyes, she could see it was *her* skin that was dark, darker than Papa's even, her hair that was coarse and curly. How could she have been so blind?

She thought Muffet was crazy to worry about the silly things she did when everything else about her was so right. Didn't she have the skin, the hair, the brains? She came from Good

Family, too. So why did she worry so about her clothes. Her complexion. Her speech. Her family. Her house. Especially her house, for there was nothing she could do about that.

But, Sadie thought, as she came back to the here and now and found herself sitting at the table in Desrine's kitchen, with the sound of oxtail browning in the pot and Desrine chopping up tomatoes and onions with her big knife, the question was not about the house but about how Desrine was supposed to look and if she looked the way she was supposed to. Desrine wasn't brown and plump and pleasing with a round face like Irene, who worked for the Turners and was called a House-keeper, if you please (as she was quick to inform everyone). Desrine wasn't elegant and pretty like Cherry, the nursemaid for the Richards girls, or lively and stylish like Clarissa.

Sadie looked at Desrine and saw a skinny black woman, but powerful, tall and skinny with not an ounce of fat on her body except for her big belly. Desrine wasn't pretty but Sadie felt comfortable with her face. She liked Desrine even though she had a long mouth. When Desrine go to vex! But Desrine was strong. Mother Dear was always saying so. You only had to look at Desrine's calves and her arms, which were heavy and muscled like a man's. There wasn't anything Desrine couldn't lift. Desrine could go on working from morning till night. Doing the cooking and the cleaning, the washing and the ironing.

But no matter how tired Desrine said she was, Sadie noticed that she never missed a visit to her children. Every two weeks, on her weekend off, she would get up early to catch the bus, or even walk all the way, to go and see her children in the bush.

Desrine never missed that. Even when the October rains started one time and fell for two weeks straight. Though they begged her to stay, even Papa, who hardly ever got involved in these things he was so busy with his papers, she still set off, wearing his big black oilskin cloak, leftover from his days at United Fruit Company, where he worked before Sadie was born. But not even that kept Desrine dry, for she had to wade through flood waters with her skirt hitched up high and her Sunday shoes hanging round her neck with the straps buckled together. She had to plough through landslides and climb over fallen trees and slip and slide on the muddy track all the way till she reached, Massa God Be Praised, though she was covered with mud from head to foot and soaked through and through.

It wasn't all sweetness and light with Desrine though, as Sadie could tell you. She was forever muttering or grumbling about something. Often she would grumble to Sadie that it's really time they get somebody to help her with the work.

"The work getting too much for one smaddy and you children getting big. Turning into young ladies. So much washing and starching and ironing to do. Going to have to talk to your mother, Sadie. Talk about getting another pair of hands." Sadie never knew if Desrine talked to Mother Dear, for hers was still the only pair of hands around their house, though nobody could say the girls didn't help out, for Mother Dear wasn't bringing up her daughters to be lazy. No sir. Nobody could say her girls didn't make their own beds and tidy their room and hang up their clothes and help with the dusting of the house on a Saturday and the cleaning of the silver and setting and clearing the table on Sunday (as

Mother Dear was always boasting to the other ladies when they came to tea). These days, Muffet didn't have much time now because she was studying to get into high school, Kingston school at that. So the whole thing fell down on Sadie. Not to mention the sewing. Mother Dear was teaching Sadie to sew. Sadie really liked sewing, but she wished every time Mother Dear pricked herself with the needle she didn't say – looking at Sadie – "That's the sign of an ungrateful child."

Mother Dear told Sadie when she longed out her mouth like Desrine that she shouldn't mind, for her turn would come to go to high school and she shouldn't be jealous of Muffet for we don't know what life will bring us all, dear, and Sadie one day would be glad she's learned to keep house and sew and cook. Oh, Mother Dear didn't make fun with them. Wanted her daughters to grow up knowing how to do things. For they weren't rich. Not like some.

Desrine was the one doing all the heavy work at their house, with Mother Dear sewing and baking and doing the accounts and running the property since Papa was so busy in his study working on his papers. Papa had never thrown out a newspaper, Mother Dear said, and Sadie believed it to be true. Papa needed the newspapers for his research, for he was writing. Sadie wasn't sure what, but she was proud of him for it made him different from the other fathers around. He was the only one who spent his day indoors, locked in his room, emerging only for meals, fussed over by Mother Dear and Desrine. Papa didn't go into the sun much but he was like the sun itself; the whole household revolved around him. The slightest distraction or annoyance would put him off his stride all week so usually Sadie and Muffet kept out of his way, speaking to him only when spoken to, which was extremely rare. Nobody liked Papa annoyed for he fussed so. Became irritable and cranky and called out to Mother Dear every five minutes because he had mislaid something. And Mother Dear would drop whatever she was doing, even if she was beating the egg whites into a meringue, even if she was pinning up a dress on one of the children, even if she was in the bathroom. Even if it was Desrine's weekend off and she was basting the chicken for dinner, she dropped everything and ran, wiping her hands on her apron, when Papa called.

Sadie noticed that Mrs. Turner, who was given to being a bit pushy (because she was the one who had made the brilliant match and lived in the big house, Muffet said), that same Mrs. Turner was very gentle with Mother Dear when the subject of Papa came up. Of course they all knew each other from long ago for they'd all grown up together in Portland where Papa's father was an Anglican minister and the girls' grandfathers had made their fortunes in bananas. But Mother Dear's father had died without making a will so everything had fallen into the hands of the Administrator General. She'd be old and grey before anything was settled, Mother Dear bitterly complained, and by then the government would have taken it all.

Mother Dear and Mrs. Turner talked about these matters all the time. About their marvellous childhoods, which made them laugh a lot, and then they would come to the subject of Papa, which made them serious. "Oh, Vivi," Mrs. Turner cried out dramatically one time. Sadie, who could hear but not see from where she was sitting at the side of the house just below the verandah, wasn't sure in response to what since nothing had been said, but was shocked to hear what sounded like sobs coming from the verandah and risked being caught by standing on tiptoe and peeping. She still couldn't see much, her eyes being on a level with the floorboards, but she could hear one of the ladies loudly blowing her nose and another saying, "Poor dear." She couldn't believe it was her mother crying. Over what, she didn't know, but the voice saying "poor dear" was unmistakably Mrs. Turner's.

Another time, she heard Mother Dear say in a low voice, "I never dreamt it would come to this. I thought marriage would have settled him down," which to Sadie seemed a strange thing to say since Papa seemed the most settled-down person she knew.

Mrs. Turner, who was never afraid to issue bold comment on every subject, even to criticizing her friend, strangely enough always held her tongue on the subject of Allen Chance.

Desrine was the one who had a great deal to say. She blamed Mother Dear for the condition he was in, "just a sickening away," as she described it, "down to him very shadow." As far as she was concerned, from the time Papa quit his good-good job "without rhyme or reason" and just started to stay home, acting strange, doing nothing, Mother Dear should have taken him to Father Whiteley so he could find Papa's spirit and put it back inside him, since it was clear as day that some wicked person had stolen it from him. Sadie was always flattered to be taken into Desrine's confidence, and though she always listened to her version of events with a sense of awe that such things were possible, it still made no sense to her, for she could not imagine her father as anything but what he was, having no remembrance of him as anything else.

"The thing is, Sadie," Desrine would say, wringing out the clothes in the wash-house, "man not suppose to spend him day inside no house. For all him do is get in the woman way, and she there trying to get on with her business. How she can get through her business if him a call-call her all the time. Man suppose to spend the day out of him yard, man. Going about him owna business. Riding around him property. Seeing that ol'nayga not tiefing him blind and that the job him hire them to do doing good. Me know what me a say, though is not everything good fe eat good fe talk. What eye don't see, heart don't grieve. But one day, story going come to bump."

Sometimes Sadie wondered and felt confused about what Desrine had to say. It was true that Mother Dear always seemed to be the one worrying about things, though she never said a word against Papa. Spent her time looking after him, protecting and defending him. The strange thing was, whenever they went out together as a family, or if there were visitors around, Mother Dear never said a word unless she was spoken to, left it up to Papa to do the talking, which he did plenty of, once he got over his initial shyness. She agreed with everything Papa said, if he asked her opinion, but ventured none of her own. It was as if Mother Dear was two selves, the one she was with Papa and the self she was with the children and Desrine and the workers on the property: the bossy self. But Mother Dear could be kind, too, never mind you saw her there so proud and haughty, Desrine said.

If you believed Desrine, Mother Dear was too kind, for every ol'nayga could come to her gate with a sad-sad story and walk away with something. "It grieve me, you see, Sadie," Desrine would complain, "how Miss Vivi make ol'nayga come fool her up. Like that Rita the other day. Come tell Miss Vivi she need the money to buy medicine for pickney. I nearly bus out laugh when I hear that and God going charge her for telling lie for He see everything. It sure to gone down in Him little book already. She will pay for it one day. For everybody know Rita want to go sport out the money. Miss Vivi will never see that shilling again."

Mother Dear was always having visits from her women workers and the wives of the labourers, visits from them or their children, was often on the back verandah listening to their stories and giving advice or helping them to sign papers and write letters, and no one left empty-handed. Mother Dear would always send lunch on Sunday to one or two of the old people around and soup to any of her poor neighbours who were sick.

"We must be kind to those less fortunate, girls," she was always telling her daughters, "as a way of giving thanks, for it is only by the grace of God that we are not in their places."

Sadie wondered if Desrine was one of the less fortunate and if this was why she was so miserable, but when she mentioned it to Muffet, Muffet said Desrine was just miserable. She couldn't stand her. It was true, Sadie thought, that Desrine wasn't a smiley-smiley sort of person and had no patience. Flew off the handle for the slightest little thing. The minute Mother Dear's back was turned, she shouted and threatened. *Mis-er-a-ble!* Muffet said. But Sadie from she was small saw through Desrine, saw that though Desrine behaved so vexed all the time, she wasn't really mad at them, perhaps she didn't even care about them one way or another. She got that feeling sometimes. Her sourness didn't have to do with them. It had to do with other things. With life, maybe. Desrine was always sighing and complaining about life. Life and her high blood pressure.

That was the only thing wrong with Desrine. Any time she got sick, sick enough to go to the doctor – and that was happening a bit too often nowadays according to Mother Dear – any time the bisi and the soursop-leaf tea ceased to help and the pain started squeezing her head again, she went to the doctor and came back and reported, first to Mother Dear and then to Sadie: "Doctor seh a the pressure again. Pressure gone up high, high, high." Sadie didn't know how the whole thing worked, but it made her feel proud to know somebody who had pressure that was "high, high, high." Only as she got older did she realize it wasn't a good thing for it could make Desrine just drop dead one day. And what would happen to her children then? Desrine worried about that a lot.

Sadie remembered how her eyes were opened that time she went with Desrine to her house, after she begged and Desrine finally said yes because she was sure her mother wouldn't let her go and she begged and begged Mother Dear till she finally threw up her hands and said, "Yes, Sadie, for God's sake, go!" When Desrine took her home, it really opened her eyes. To see Desrine laugh and love up her children, hug and kiss and cuddle them! Muffet never believed her, never believed miserable old Desrine could have nice ways, much less feelings.

The funny thing is (and Sadie didn't tell Muffet this part), the funny thing is, the minute they walked out to the road and got on *Confidence* to return home the Sunday evening, Desrine just shed that new self. The laughing and happy self. In the twinkling of an eye Desrine's mouth long out again and her face set up. Not a word did she speak for the entire way. Desrine just got off the bus and walked to their house with the box of ground provisions her father sent for Mother Dear, his best yams and sweet potatoes and plantains, walked with the box of food on her head and her two long hands at her side, walked straight, looking neither to the left nor to the right, behaving as if Sadie wasn't there. She went straight round to the back of the house and pitched the box down on the table on the back verandah. Sadie knew she could see the family inside the living room, see them clear as anything through the glass, but she never called out, "How di do." She never even said "goodnight" to Sadie, who had followed her onto the back verandah. She didn't say even "Dog!" to Sadie. She just marched to her cottage and slammed the door. Didn't even bother to light the lamp. Not a light showed in the crack of her door, for Sadie stood there silently on the back verandah as night fell, looking at Desrine's door and wondering, is what trouble her ee? Till suddenly she realized she was standing alone in the darkness and in a panic she rushed round to the front verandah and pounded on the door, calling out: "Mother Dear, I'm home. Please, Mam. Quick. Open the door."

᎓ ᎓

At first Sadie was worried that Manuela's absence had something to do with her and what had taken place in the arbour last year, but she quickly dismissed that idea. After all, Manuela had been as guilty as she, worse, for Manuela had forgotten her place; it was something she would never have dared tell her mother about. But Desrine had come back from her last visit home in a terrible state, and Sadie knew right away it had to do with Manuela, for Desrine got so angry when Sadie asked about her. The next morning Sadie could see that Desrine had something important to tell Mother Dear, so she was paying more attention than usual to the two women, not to be faas (as Muffet would say if she knew) but so she could find out what was happening to Manuela.

Sadie had noticed Desrine's eyes were red that morning, as if she had been crying. Not that anybody would ever see Desrine cry: big people never liked you to know they can cry, except the time Mother Dear got the letter from Aunt Mim in Kingston saying she and Uncle Edward had decided to take the girls, starting with Muffet, so they could go to high school, for she and Uncle Edward don't have children of their own, that's exactly what Aunt Mim said in the letter, for Mother Dear was reading it out loud in the living room after supper, and right in the middle of reading it, she burst into tears. Papa lent her his handkerchief and patted her shoulder and she was smiling though she was crying, everybody could see that, so nobody felt sad and she said, "I'm so happy because a great burden has been lifted from my shoulders: how to school my girls." That's what Mother Dear told them before she made them kneel right down on the living-room linoleum and say a prayer to thank God for Aunt Mim and Uncle Edward though it wasn't time for prayers.

A lot of praying and thanking God and crying went on that night, for when Sadie and Muffet went to their room, Muffet started to cry. Sadie got up and sat on the edge of Muffet's bed and said, "What's the matter?" Muffet threw her arms around her and said, "Oh, Sadie, I'm so happy, I'm going away to school," and kept right on crying into Sadie's nightdress, but it was crying for joy so, after a time, Sadie went back to her own bed. Sadie didn't bother to cry for joy for in the back of her mind there was already the nagging feeling that she would never get to go to Kingston and live with Aunt Mim and Uncle Edward and ride on tram cars and go to the movies and Hope Gardens and eat ice cream every Sunday. That Aunt Mim would find some excuse for not taking her. For Aunt Mim already found so much fault with her. Every time Aunt Mim's name was mentioned, Sadie's stomach churned and she was cast back to the day she listened when she shouldn't have and heard Aunt Mim pronounce with finality, "Sadie takes after the other side of the family. Sadie could easily turn down." Sadie switched her mind back to the present, back to Desrine's daughter who was the one who had turned down.

Sadie could never say she actually saw Desrine crying but she was extremely upset the day she burst out with the news.

Sadie just happened to be standing outside the dining-room window (accidentally on purpose, Muffet would have said) because both Mother Dear and Desrine were lingering after breakfast so Sadie knew something was up. But she nearly died with fright when she heard the actual news. Her ears had pricked up when she heard Desrine exclaim: "Miss Vivi, I shame. Shame till a turn fool. Shame to tell you what that Manuela do me, me who working out mi soul-case so pay good money give her lesson so she can turn somebody and hold her head up high. So she can turn round and help me with them other one lef a yard. You know what Manuela do me, Miss Vivi?"

"Desrine, for Heaven's sake! Don't tell me Manuela is expecting?" Mother Dear's voice was sharp.

"As God is me witness, Miss Vivi. Manuela go get herself in the way."

In the way! Sadie felt the blood rush to her head. She was amazed. She thought only big people could make baby and Manuela wasn't big people never mind she got breasts before Muffet.

"For goodness' sake!" she heard Mother Dear say. "What is the matter with these little girls, eh? When did this happen?"

"Miss Vivi, I don't know, for I never consider seh Manuela reach the age where she even have them kind of knowledge. Never dream so at all. Think she is still little pickney going to lesson. How me fe stay clear down here and know she turn big woman?"

"So how far gone is she?"

"Miss Vivi, you see me here? I can't tell you nutten. I don't want even Manuela name mention in mi hearing for is that mek mi pressure rise. Me tell you, if it wasn't for her grandfather there tek her and hide her away, pick up the girl and run with her into the bush, I would kill her there the day. Is her old grandfather save her. For is machete I grab up. I can't even remember when I do that. Is look down I look down when I come to my senses, and I see I holding machete. Miss Vivi, mi heart still full to think that girl could cause me to do such a terrible thing, kill mi own flesh and blood. I so vex, I had was to leave the house same time. Walk come straight back here. Never even remember mi head-tie. Heart so grieve, can't even tell you how I walk it or who I pass or how I reach or where my pressure gone to."

When she paused for breath, Mother Dear said, "Poor Desrine. You try so hard with those children. So your mother wasn't keeping a good eye on her?"

"Me don't know what to say. Miss Mary swear to Massa God Manuela never go any place except to lesson and come straight home every day. Say she know where Manuela was every minute. I don't know what to think. Miss Vivi, I can't tell you how mi heart grieve. Bad enough she making baby, but it look like this one going come without father for she don't name anyone. So is me same one going have to mind it. Don't ask if girl pickney not crosses."

"Desrine, maybe I shouldn't say it, but is same way you started young," Mother Dear said. "Seven of them you have. With no father to mind them. You took a heavy burden on yourself and it looks as if Manuela is following right in your footsteps."

"Miss Vivi, I don't want you to think I impertinent, Mam, I never impertinence off to you yet, but that is very unfair," Desrine retorted. "You could never say I run around. Is only two baby-father I have. I never run up and down and get those children. Two so-so gentleman."

"But seven of them, Desrine?"

"Don't is Massa God decide how much is my lot? Nuh him give me my knot? You want me to fly in the face of God and say, I don't want no more pickney? Don't untie all my knot? Is sickness you want me to have? You want me was to dash them weh before they born and turn my body into graveyard? If they come, Miss Vivi, you have to take them for is yours."

"Desrine, I don't know why I bother to try and reason with you. But what is going to happen with Manuela?"

"Well, me just have to leave her to her Granny for the time being. There is nothing I can do. How much time you see me have to spend with those children? Don't is their Granny raise them? All me poor gal do is work and send them mi wages. Nuh so life stay?"

"I just don't understand you people at all. But Desrine, I don't want the girls to know anything about what has happened to Manuela, do you hear me? I don't want my children to grow up faster than their years. Not a word, you hear? Especially to that Sadie. I worry enough about her as it is."

Sadie pricked up her ears at that and felt her face grow hot and her head grow big, but to her great disappointment, nothing more was said. Desrine said, "Yes, Miss Vivi," in a resigned sort of voice and Sadie could hear the chair scrape as Mother Dear got up from the table.

"Worry enough!" Sadie wondered: what does Mother Dear mean?

But the news about Manuela pushed everything else out of Sadie's mind, especially when she told Muffet and Muffet said that Manuela's belly was going to swell up now because it had a seed growing inside.

"Muffet, you lie! You mean a seed that's going to turn into a tree?"

"Just like a tree."

Sadie knew if you swallowed guinep seed it would grow inside you, turn into a tree, and burst right through your head. Everybody knew that. Mother Dear was always warning them to be careful not to swallow guinep seed. Why would she warn them if it wasn't true? The tree would just take root. And who would want a daughter walking around the place with a tree growing through the top of her head? You think that would look nice to other people? Your mother would be ashamed, man, to have such a daughter.

That's what Sadie said to the other girls when they discussed the matter at recess, all of them standing in a tight little circle in the schoolyard with guineps weighing down their pinafore pockets, cracking the skins with their teeth, popping the juicy guineps into their mouths, allowing the sweetness to melt out of sight of Mrs. Mighty, putting the seeds and crisp broken shells back in their pockets to be disposed of outside the schoolyard so Mrs. Mighty would have no evidence to convict them, Mrs. Mighty the Deputy in her crepe-sole shoes who would corn their bottoms for them if only she knew.

"Ashamed, man, to have a daughter like that," Sadie told her avid listeners. "How your mother could hold up her head in church and Mothers Union and when she taking tea with the other ladies and in front of her big important sister in Kingston married to big-big lawyer? And her daughter such a sight to behold? Making an exhibition of herself. Everybody would be talking."

Sadie tried to remember what happened when Desrine herself had her babies, if she looked as if she had swallowed something, but she couldn't remember noticing anything special about Desrine, whose belly was big all the time anyway. Desrine would just go away for two weeks' holidays, and long afterwards, Sadie would hear by accident that she had a new little baby at home.

Whatever was happening to Manuela, Sadie felt sorry for her, especially if her belly was going to swell up and she had to take to her bed, for Manuela didn't like that sort of thing at all, she could never sit still. If you let her, Manuela would spend the whole day running up and down like mad-ants. Nothing Manuela liked better than chat-chat and faas and play games. She was as restless as Sadie. Even when she was sitting down, Manuela's body would move like she was dancing.

Despite her amazement, Sadie couldn't help feeling a grudging kind of admiration for Manuela, for only bad girls got babies when they were young. That's what the teachers and everybody said when another big girl dropped out of school. And now, when Sadie thought about it, she decided that that Manuela was bad in truth, she was rotten through and through. Look how she had showed herself so two-faced to Sadie that day in the arbour last summer!

Sadie was sure Manuela had liked her the first time they met, when Desrine had taken Sadie to her house. Oh, Manuela had been all over Sadie then. Couldn't stop making much of her. Untied Sadie's long hair and replaited it endlessly. Over and over she had combed out Sadie's long hair which was like wet sugar pouring into the pan to set, wet sugar when it's full of molasses and pouring in waves. Manuela said that while the other children gathered round with their eyes open wide, looking at Sadie bask in their adoration. They knew just what Manuela meant, for they had all at one time or another gone down to Mister Raymond's sugar mill in the valley and watched as he slowly poured the wet sugar into the shut-pan, wet sugar full of molasses.

They had spent practically one whole morning sitting on the bench under the almond tree playing with Sadie's hair and stroking her skin, holding their arms against hers and comparing. Sadie's skin was smooth, the colour of logwood honey, and she had freckles across her nose that were much admired. Everybody thought Sadie was the most beautiful creature they had ever laid eyes on, with her long eyelashes and everything, though Sadie herself didn't think anything of the sort. That wasn't the view she had of herself at all, not when she was at home.

At home, Sadie's hair was such a bother. It was too long and thick for her to manage, so they had to get her a big, heavy comb, not like the fine little comb Muffet used, a proper tortoiseshell comb that came with the comb-and-brush set that could sit so prettily on the doily on top of the vanity. No, Sadie had to have a bakelite comb with huge teeth like what people like Desrine used and which she made sure to hide in the back of her drawer the minute Mother Dear finished combing her hair every morning. She would have died if anyone came to their house and saw the class of comb Mother Dear had to use on her daughter's head and Mother Dear's mother an English lady with dead-straight hair. Muffet had come with good hair like Mother Dear's. But fine and straight. So she could just let it out long and flowing loose under her hat looking so nice when they went to church on Sunday.

Sadie couldn't manage her own hair. Imagine! It was so bad. Next thing, she would let that hair get loose, man. Like letting out a wild beast to run all over the world, scaring clouds and knocking down mountains and overturning rocks and getting tangled in trees and falling into rivers and getting stuck in brambles and heaven knows what else. Cutting it short didn't help. Mother Dear tried. What a disaster! It came like dry coconut husk. You know coir? Like bush. Like any old macca you see there springing up in the pasture. Frizzed up right round her head. Muffet said she looked just like her Golliwog and laughed, for it was a joke, but Sadie didn't laugh, she thought it was a terrible insult to compare her to anything so black and ugly and couldn't understand how her very own sister could say such a hurtful thing like that. Everybody thought she was crying because she didn't like her hair cut short. But in fact, she liked the way it made her look wild and different,

different from everybody else. Liked the way she could stand in front of the mirror and shake it to make it shimmy. Liked to run her hand through it and feel it's waviness. Liked the shape of her head. But Mother Dear prayed for her hair to grow back so it could be controlled by plaits, kept under restraint by ribbons and hairclips.

Mother Dear never said a word when she was busy fighting with the hair, though she made sounds like *hmmph*, little grunts like that from time to time. Every daughter of mine is going to turn out properly, Sadie could imagine Mother Dear thinking furiously as, with the hair captured and subdued, rolled into two and pinned up, she could now safely take hold of each section and begin to plait. Every one (plait). Even those (plait) who acted (plait) like they belonged (plait, plait) in the fish-vendors' side (plait) of Mo Bay market (plait, plait). She never said a word out loud but Sadie knew what she was thinking. For she did say things aloud sometimes and Sadie had big ears. Little remarks to Muffet or Mrs. Turner, or Aunt Mim when she came. So if Sadie ran all these things together in her head, brought together all the little scraps, it would be like a long ribbon of sound that came and went, came and went, zig-zagging like the waves in Sadie's hair and Mother Dear like a mermaid rising up on the crest of each wave saying: No! Not even from my own daughter, never mind can't help certain things. Not her fault at all. If only poor Mother Chance wasn't so – before falling back in the trough, defeated.

The worst part was that even though Mother Dear never said a word when she combed Sadie's hair, Sadie imagined that Muffet knew every word she was likely to say, for she lived in the same house, didn't she? She had ears, too. Knew every word of Sadie's shame.

But that time at Desrine's house, with Mother Dear and Muffet and Aunt Mim and all the society ladies far, far away, nobody could say Sadie wasn't enjoying the attention she was receiving from Desrine's children and everybody else. All that attention was making her feel good, man. People fussing over her. Fussing and talking about her loud as if she wasn't there, but nice! The children and Mass Eustace and Miss Mary and everybody, even strangers coming into their yard who never before set eyes on Sadie talking nice, saying how Sadie sweet-sweet. Sadie was a darling! That's what the big people said, the old men and all. What a pretty little darling! Oh Sadie!

Of course when Manuela came to their house, they would never have dreamed of taking her with them when they went visiting. But it was all right to take her to Sunday School. Yet the very first time Manuela had gone to church with them, Sadie felt so ashamed to be seen with her, had acted so badly, it still made her feel uncomfortable whenever she remembered it. She used to dream about it and wake up sweating. She had started to worry even before Sunday School ended and they went into church for the regular service, worry because she didn't want Manuela sitting in church beside them. Sadie usually enjoyed church, enjoyed seeing everything and being seen and greeting people afterwards. But not this day. Right near the end of Sunday School which was held under the big saman tree in the churchyard, it all turned to ashes in her mouth, for she suddenly realized that Manuela would follow them in when big church started. Follow them right to their pew. And she couldn't bear the thought of having Manuela sit beside them, for what would people think? What if Mrs. Turner came to church? Or Mr. and Mrs. Richards? What on earth would they think when they saw this black girl in her old clothes sitting right there next to Sadie? They would know for sure that Sadie was just like all those no-count people. Know she was not one of *them*. She would never be invited to enter their front door again. They would talk right through her. She would become as invisible as the servants. Sadie knew she was going to *die* with Desrine's daughter sitting right up there in front with them.

But, as it turned out, Manuela didn't come to sit with them. So Sadie spent the whole service worrying about that, worrying that Manuela was vexed that Sadie had cut her eye at her and rushed off and left her under the tree. Manuela didn't know a soul and here was Sadie rushing off and leaving her like that. Sadie worried that maybe Manuela had gone home and told Desrine, and now Desrine would be mad. But when service was over and Sadie turned around to look at the congregation, she saw Manuela sitting at the very back. She felt so relieved that Manuela hadn't taken offence or come to sit beside them, she made a point of walking side by side with Manuela all the way home, so everyone could see she wasn't stuck-up. She decided that the minute she got home she would make Manuela a present of an old perfume bottle which Manuela so admired for its shape and a long-lost scent which she insisted she could still discern. Sadie remembered how Manuela had seemed so childish and silly that day playing with the perfume bottle. Yet here she was, making baby.

— —

It seemed to Sadie that everything was happening at once. Summer had almost ended, Manuela was making baby, and Muffet was about to leave for high school. Desrine and Mother Dear were both worrying. Sadie couldn't see any difference between the two when it came to worrying. Mother Dear had a husband, it is true, and Desrine had none, and some of the things they wanted might be different. Mother Dear didn't have to worry like Desrine did about having a roof over her head one day, her own little house where she could be with her children. And Desrine didn't have to worry like Mother Dear about whether she could unpick one of her gowns to remake it into a dress for Muffet to wear to Maria Dolores's party and whether it would take a blue dye to hide the worn spots. But they both worried all the time about finding money for school uniforms and school fees and extra lessons, about giving the children a good start in life.

Both of them worrying, worrying so much, it all added up to the same thing. One day Mother Dear went to the doctor and he told her what he'd been telling Desrine for years. She had high blood pressure.

Of course Mother Dear wouldn't come home and tell a thing like that to her children; oh, children were never told anything, but Sadie found out, for Desrine couldn't wait to pass on the information.

"Sadie, you know seh yu mother get pressure, too? Yes, girl," Desrine said gleefully, for this was news. "Now she will understand what I been going through, for rockstone a river bottom never know sun hot. But, girl, how this house going manage with two people with pressure in it, Massa God him one know. Two pressure-sufferer! But me could tell from long time is that she did have, you know? She never have no need for Doctor. With all her worries, is just a big surprise Miss Vivi never get pressure before. Girl, Doctor say her pressure gone up high, high, high. But it still not as high as mine!"

Mother Dear was busier than ever, sewing clothes for Muffet. Although it was only the uniforms that Aunt Mim expected her to sew, for she said she would outfit Muffet with everything else, Mother Dear didn't think that was good enough.

"Muffet is my daughter after all," she could be heard telling Desrine. "My daughter. No matter how Miss Mim says she will mind her, and I know she will, I must send her off with a good wardrobe to take shame out of my eyes."

"True word, Miss Vivi," Desrine agreed. "Miss Muff must leave here with full suitcase. Can't send her off with her two so-so hand. People would talk, man. Whole trunk she must leave here with go a railway station. Heavy, heavy trunk. People must see that she leave here with tings."

Sadie felt sad that Muffet would be going, for though she could be so serious and unyielding sometimes, though she made Sadie cry, Sadie still had a great deal of admiration for one so certain of her path, and she couldn't imagine what life would be like without her. Even if Sadie were to join Muffet in Kingston, if Aunt Mim did send for her, she knew that by then Muffet would have moved even further beyond her, for Muffet was now saying she intended to work real hard in school so she could win a scholarship and go away to university. This totally amazed Sadie, for she couldn't think of a single person she knew who had been to university. Well, Papa's father, the Reverend Chance, had gone to university, so they said. And mad old Reverend Prothero. But they were old white men from England and Anglican ministers at that. Women couldn't be ministers, only men were ministers. White men from England who always seemed to be tall and bony or short and fat and talked in a braying kind of way and had cold, dry hands when they shook yours after service or patted your head, and ate a great deal, a very great deal if your mother had the good fortune (she said) to have them for lunch the Sunday they came to preach at your church, ate so much there was never any chicken with bread-and-sage stuffing (Sadie's favourite) left over for supper.

So what gave Muffet the idea that she could go to university like these old white men? University was far away. Over the seas to England. Or Canada. Or America. Why did Muffet want to leave home and go so far? If Muffet were rich, she wouldn't have to bother about getting an education. The Delvallie and the Richards girls didn't. Because as soon as they left boarding school they would get husbands. That's what girls like them got. Most of the girls at elementary school with Sadie wouldn't get husbands. They would get babies. Like Manuela. That's just how the world was. Only the better-off girls, the ones who wore shoes, were headed for high school.

But that Muffet had to be different. She said she was going to get an education. And a husband. And babies. Sadie wasn't sure what she herself would get, she didn't know if she wanted a husband. Or babies. But what else was there? She could be like her class teacher, Miss Theobalds, who also taught Sunday School. Miss Theobalds had an education but didn't have husband or child. So people laughed at Miss Theobalds who was flat as a cassava wafer. Called her Old Maid. Called her Mule. Even Sadie, when she was hanging out with the barefoot children at school. Miss Theobalds had her own house and her own piano and a big black ladies-wheel Raleigh which she rode to school. Sang like an angel. Trained the church choir. And the school choir. Miss Theobalds was very "delicate." Mrs. Mighty always said so when two days every month Miss Theobalds sent a note by a passing child to say she was sick and couldn't come to school which left Mrs. Mighty taking two classes at a time. Of course that didn't mean a thing to Mrs. Mighty, for there was nothing that woman couldn't do; she certainly knew how to "handle children." That's what everybody said. The children themselves whispered it on the playground when somebody was being particularly rude ("You can gwan, till Miz Mighty ketch you. Miz Mighty don't make fun to *handle children!*") Mrs. Mighty had an education and a husband and several children of her own who had already passed through her hands. Mrs. Mighty was big and mighty as her name, with her crepe-sole shoes and her loud voice and her leather strap. Sadie certainly didn't want to be like Mrs. Mighty either.

Mother Dear was always telling Sadie she should be like Muffet and put her head to the books, how else did she expect to get anywhere? But Sadie didn't bother. She didn't study hard but she was doing well at school anyway. Not as well as Muffet, of course, for everybody knew Muffet was Big Brains. But Sadie never failed anything yet, that's one thing. Not like that Manuela.

Sometimes Sadie thought with satisfaction of how dumb that Manuela was, how Manuela couldn't even read properly and her writing resembled crab-toe. Whenever Sadie thought of her superiority in this area, it made her feel better, and she told herself that she would beat the books so she could turn out as smart as Muffet. But soon she'd forget about being better than Manuela or as good as Muffet, and she'd go back to playing marbles with the boys in the schoolyard.

Sadie knew that she would never play with Manuela and Muffet together again, that all the foolishness they used to go on with in the granadilla arbour, that Queendom of Hyacinth business, was over. That Muffet and Manuela were set on their own separate paths. And she? What would she be? Sadie couldn't tell, and that always made her angry. It was all because of her hair that her life was so confusing, she now decided. Her hair was turning her into a ragamuffin. Muffet had been right. Who ever saw a princess with a natty head? Her nayga hair and her darkened skin were what had made her stoop so low as to play with that stupid Manuela. Yes, Sadie decided. To consider having her as a friend. That Manuela wasn't a nice person at all and Sadie was glad she was never coming to her house again. Look at how she had behaved to Sadie that time down in the arbour, that very Sadie who was the one who had brought her into the bosom of her family. You think that after all Sadie did for Manuela, Manuela should treat Sadie so the minute Muffet smiled at her, cut her eye at Sadie? Start playing with Muffet and admiring her can't done? Behaving as if she don't even know Sadie again?

Don't think Sadie was so vexed, every time they started up that foolishness in the granadilla arbour, Manuela saying she's opening hairdressing parlour and that stupid Muffet going right along with her, going to have her hair done, swishing in with Mother Dear's handbag and long skirt, carrying comb and bobby pins and hairpins and wearing Mother Dear's big hat. That Manuela was in her element and Sadie was ashamed of her big sister Muffet. The one that everyone said was so bright? The one who was going off to high school in Kingston so should know better? To see that girl acting such a fool! For even after Sadie said she thought it was a stupid game, Muffet still said she wanted to play. Sadie would run off and leave them, to play by herself or go and bother Mother Dear or Desrine. Once she'd even crept back down to where they were playing and climbed up the mango tree and shaken the arbour and frightened them. It rained down leaves and twigs and lizards and unripe granadillas as they screamed. She didn't care.

After that she stayed away for a while. But no matter where Sadie went, she could still hear them laughing down in the granadilla arbour, laughing fit to kill, even Muffet, who wasn't used to laughing out loud unless that Manuela was about. It was hard to keep away with people laughing and making noise in your head like that. So Sadie went back down to the arbour.

There was that Manuela, with her head wrapped in Desrine's head-tie like a turban, greeting her customers in this speaky-spokey voice, behaving as if she were a beautician, though you wonder how Manuela living in her bush could ever know about these things.

"Good morning, Madame Sarsaparilla," Muffet was calling out to Manuela.

"Oh, the Princess Lapidalapida! From the Queendom of Hyacinths. And how is the Queen today?" Manuela exclaimed, for that is how Muffet said they should be addressed and she liked to play different parts. "How wonderful to see my illustrious customer." (Oh, that was Muffet's coaching all right, Sadie thought.) "Do sit down, Your Royal Highness."

Muffet sat on the flat rock that was Manuela's chair. "See that you do a good job this time," she said, "or else it will be off with your head!"

Don't ask if that Manuela didn't have fun, combing out Muffet's hair. Combing it with Muffet's little fine-tooth tortoiseshell comb and playing with it and pinning it up with the bobby pins, pinning it up and taking it down again. All the time exclaiming how pretty it was. How fine it was. How beautiful it was. What lovely fine skin Muffet had. So white!

The day Sadie went back to play with them she sat there till she felt fit to burst. Suddenly she shot up from the ground where she was sitting, pulled off her ribbons and undid her plaits, went outside, shook her hair loose, and came back inside the arbour and announced herself: "Her Royal Majesty, the Countess of ChinChin."

Muffet giggled.

"Welcome, Countess," Manuela said, laughing too. "What can I do for you?"

"I would like to have my hair done, Madame Sarsaparilla, the same as the Princess Lapidalapida. A nice upsweep. We're all going to the ball. Prince Charming, you know."

"Would you take a seat, Countess, on this lovely couch, and I will deal with you as soon as I am finished with the Princess Lapidalapida."

"Very well," said Sadie, making herself comfortable on the ground again and beginning to enjoy the joke.

Well, up to now Sadie couldn't believe that Manuela could be so bad-minded. Bold and wicked and bad-minded. For when Manuela was finished with Muffet's hair and it was Sadie's turn, and she went and sat on the big rock which was Manuela's chair, hear what this Manuela did. She lifted up Sadie's thick, heavy hair, lifted it up and ran her fingers through it. Then she said, very, very, disdainfully, "Oh, I am so sorry, Countess, but we don't do this kind of hair in this parlour."

"What do you mean?" Sadie asked. Speaking as Sadie, not as the Countess. But Manuela was pretending she was Madame Sarsaparilla still. Speaking in the speaky-spokey voice she adopted for the Madame which made Muffet laugh. She said: "This kind of hair needs straightening. This is bad hair. We don't do straightening here."

"Straightening!" Sadie shrieked.

"Oh yes, Countess. It's not straight at all."

"Bad hair!" Sadie yelled again.

"Sadie!" Muffet said in her prim voice.

"Well, yes," said Manuela. "We only do white people's hair in this parlour. Nice straight hair. You'll have to go down the road to Madame Blackadoodoo."

"White people!" Sadie screamed. "Madam Blackadoo-doo!"

To Sadie's amazement, Muffet shrieked with laughter, the same Muffet that was always putting Manuela in her place. Muffet's laugh made Manuela scream with laughter, too. Open-mouthed, Sadie stared at the two of them cackling away in the arbour. Laughing at her. She couldn't believe it. Couldn't believe that that Manuela could be so bold. That same barefoot, picky-head, bungo, nayga-gal Manuela who not so long ago was playing in this self-same hair on Sadie's head and saying it's so beautiful. Running her hand over Sadie's arms and saying her skin's so beautiful. Now she's telling Sadie she has bad hair and must go on down the road? To Madame Blackadoodoo? Boy! Sadie just went for Manuela. Leapt up and gave Manuela such a box it made her reel.

"How dare you!" Sadie was as shocked to hear the sound of her slap on Manuela's face as the sound of her voice so hard and cold. She felt her own face burn and she looked at her hand in astonishment, she who had never before struck anyone. Out of the corner of her eye she saw Manuela pull herself together and clench her fist, and she shut her eyes tight, fully expecting Manuela to hit her back. But nothing happened and she opened her eyes to see Manuela standing there, breathing hard, but with all expression wiped from her face, looking exactly the way she looked when Desrine slapped her. Manuela was standing there with her eyes drawn way back into her head, like she wasn't seeing Sadie at all. Sadie felt tears come into her eyes, and she might have said something to Manuela then and there, something like "I'm sorry," if Muffet hadn't spoken. She had forgotten for a moment about Muffet, everything had happened so fast. Muffet had two bright spots on her cheeks, a sign that she was mad. But she wasn't mad at Manuela.

"Sadie! You should be ashamed of yourself," she hissed. "Behaving so common. Behaving like a marketwoman. Letting this little black girl drag you down. As if you don't know any better. You're just as bad as she is."

Sadie dropped her eyes and felt shame shoot right through her down to her toes. Down to her very footbottom. Muffet had said it. Said it was that Manuela bringing out this badness in her. Bringing out this badness and causing her to act like *cuffee*. Like *bungo*. Like *quashie*. Like *nayga*. Like *boogooyaga*. Causing her to turn down. She stood up straight and cut her eye at that Manuela and vowed she would never, ever speak to her again. Never speak to that stupid barefoot Manuela who was now standing there in the arbour looking stiff with fright. Good! Frightened like anything since Muffet spoke to her like that. Good! Frightened because she knows she's forgotten her place. Oh yes, Miss. Frightened because she doesn't know what's going to happen to her, ee-hee, now! Suppose they tell her mother what she dared to say to Sadie? Ta-ra! Dog would surely nyam her supper. Oh yes, Miss! Manuela's going to wet her pants from worry. The thought made Sadie feel a hundred times better. Until she looked at Muffet who had been gathering up her things and was now standing at the entrance to the arbour, dressed in Mother Dear's clothes but looking not at all foolish. Standing there and looking at the two of them with the utmost scorn. "Sadie, are you coming?" she asked, in Mother Dear's voice. Sadie looked at Muffet; then she couldn't help it, she turned and looked at Manuela. Manuela had unwound the turban from her head and was very slowly and very carefully folding it into tinier and tinier squares. Sadie stood there mesmerized by Manuela's action, unable to move, wanting to see how small a square Manuela could make from Desrine's headtie, as if it were the most important thing in the world.

"Stay here, then, now you've found your place," said Muffet, her voice like a lash. She skinned up her nose at the two of them and swept out of the arbour.

Feeling tired and confused, Sadie sat down on the rock, ignoring Manuela. Then she realized her hair was loose and she had to plait it back. But when she touched it, she found that her hair was totally out of control now, had turned into a wild animal. A *leggo beas*! She struggled but she couldn't manage it, until she got so angry and frustrated she started to bawl. In her misery, she heard rather than saw Manuela move, and felt her take hold of her hair, separate it with her fingers and plait it into two tight plaits the way it was before. Plaited it tight till it hurt. But neither of them uttered a word. When Manuela was finished, they both got up without looking at one another and left the arbour and went their separate ways, Sadie heading for the big house and Manuela for the kitchen and Desrine.

— —

Now that Muffet had gone and there was nobody to play with, now that she knew Manuela could no longer be a part of her life, Sadie couldn't even think of anything to ask Desrine about. She felt totally uncurious. It was as if she too was changing, was settling into being a quieter, less boisterous person, no longer wanting to shock or kick pupalicks or utter dirty rhymes. Desrine, too, seemed to have less than usual to say, often so lost in her own thoughts she couldn't be bothered to quarrel with Sadie or even to half-heartedly chase her out of the kitchen as she used to do. At first, Sadie thought Desrine was still sad about Manuela, but when she did speak, it turned out she was busily making plans for when the baby was born. She now sounded pleased to be having a grandchild, something to boast about to the other women. Sadie had even overheard her saying to Cherry (who had no children as yet) how satisfied she was that her daughter had proved herself, shown she was not a mule. Sadie had to smile at how the news gave Desrine one up on that little wire-waist Cherry.

Sadie began to wish she had someone to boast about her like that, for it seemed no matter what Manuela did, or failed to do, Desrine still felt pride in her. Mother Dear never acted like that to Sadie, or so it seemed, especially since, with Muffet gone, Sadie had expected to be showered with attention. But Mother

Dear seemed more preoccupied and anxious than ever with the property, the accounts, the house, Papa's needs, and nothing Sadie did seemed to please. Now her favourite line was "Sadie, how can I send you to your Aunt Mim with your hair looking like bush?" Or "How can I send you to your Aunt Mim when you are looking so black? Why can't you stay out of the sun?" Or "How can I send you to your Aunt Mim if you don't practise speaking properly?" Sadie began to dread hearing the very name of Aunt Mim.

As Manuela's time drew near, Desrine's mouth began to long out more than ever. She complained incessantly of "bad feelings," of having no one to help her in the house, of having to work out in people's yard and not be able to watch her grandchildren grow. More and more Desrine talked of leaving. She had often mentioned this to Sadie, whenever she was feeling displeased, but for the first time since Sadie had known her, she had a definite plan. She said that as soon as Manuela had the baby, Manuela could go out and find work, for she was too young to stay home. She, Desrine, would go and mind Manuela's baby, for her mother Miss Mary was getting too old for that now. They would manage somehow. She was busily petitioning Mr. Turner and Mr. Richards, the big estate owners, to give jobs to Jason and Sam, the two older boys who were now fifteen and sixteen. She was planning to send Mikey for extra lessons, for she had switched her educational hopes to him.

Sadie didn't know if this was just more of Desrine's talk, but she found herself having the same dream over and over. It wasn't like her usual fantastic dreams, in colour. This one was always in black and white and was as clear as day.

Sadie dreamed Desrine's daughter Manuela had come to show the baby to Desrine. Manuela led a procession of Desrine's children whose names Sadie couldn't remember, but they all came in one long line, each wearing a silvery turban, each carrying a sprig of green bush in one hand and a lighted candle in the other. Sadie was standing right there at the gate with Desrine as they came on in stately file but they all looked right through her, as if she was invisible. One by one they saluted Desrine and, as each one came up and bowed, Desrine placed on each child's head a box in which she had placed some of her possessions. Each child stood up with the box balanced on his or her head, wheeled around and set off in procession the way they had come, led by Manuela and the baby, their bare feet skimming the ground. As the last child turned and left with the final box, Sadie was astonished to see Desrine fall in right behind them, with nothing left to carry except for her changepurse and her handkerchief, which she always pushed down into her bosom. She went striding down the road with her two long hands at her side, looking neither to the left nor to the right. Desrine wasn't wearing her head-tie or her hat. Her hair had been straightened and her curls gleamed in the sun. By now Mother Dear had walked out to the gate to watch the procession, but Desrine had said nothing to her in farewell. Nor did she answer Sadie when she called out, "Goodbye, Desrine." Desrine had looked right through her. Sadie started running down the road behind Desrine and the string of children but her legs soon became mired in what seemed like a bog clotted with water hyacinths and she had to struggle so hard to lift each foot from the mud and the invasive rootstalk and floating bladder-like stems, she couldn't keep up. She was crying and crying in frustration, struggling to extricate herself when, faintly, she heard Mother Dear's voice calling. She turned in her direction and saw Mother Dear throw her a huge comb. She caught the comb and immediately felt her feet coming out of the bog which was drying up so rapidly, the water hyacinths shrinking, in an instant she was standing on firm roadway again. Now she had lost the desire to follow Desrine. She nevertheless turned to watch her disappear down the road, waiting for her to spin around and wave, so she could go back to Mother Dear. But until Desrine got too small to be seen, she never looked back.

Acknowledgements

Earlier versions of some of these stories appeared in *Kunapipi* (Denmark) and *Matatu* (Germany). I am grateful to the Hawthornden Foundation for a fellowship to Hawthornden Castle International Retreat for Writers – to Diana Bailey, Joan Goody, Jan Michael, and George Dickson in Britain and the Netherlands and the Harris and Thomas families in Portugal for making home not seem so far away, to Mervyn Morris, Velma Pollard, Victor Chang, and Evelyn O'Callaghan for reading and commenting on parts of the manuscript at various times, to Peter Buck for his keen eye, and, above all, to Ellen Seligman, best of editors.

Olive Senior was born and brought up in Jamaica, and has worked in journalism both in Canada and Jamaica. She is the author of three highly acclaimed collections of short fiction, *Summer Lightning*, winner of the 1987 Commonwealth Writers Prize; *Arrival of the Snake-Woman*; and *Discerner of Hearts*. She is also the author of two poetry collections, *Talking of Trees* and *Gardening in the Tropics*, and non-fiction books, including *Working Miracles: Women's Lives in the English-speaking Caribbean*.

Senior has been writer-in-residence at the University of Alberta, the Banff International Writing Studio, and the University of the West Indies, as well as an Arts Council of England visiting international writer and a Dana Distinguished Professor of Creative Writing and International Education, St. Lawrence University, Canton, New York. She has taught writing workshops in many places, including the Humber School for Writers at Humber College; the University of Toronto; the University of Miami, Florida; the University of the West Indies in Jamaica and Barbados; and Barnard College, New York.

When she is not travelling, Olive Senior lives in Toronto.